Gold, Frankincense & Myrrh

A TALE OF LOVE, MAGIC AND A MIRACLE OR TWO

A novel by

Ed Okonowicz

Gold, Frankincense & Myrrh

First Edition

ISBN 1-890690-20-1
ISBN 13 978-1-890690-20-5

This is a work of fiction. The names and incidents are products of the author's imagination, are used fictitiously and are not to be construed as real. Any similarity to actual persons, living or dead—or events, locales, business establishments or organizations—is coincidental or accidental. Some familiar settings have been used, but the events associated with these sites, as well as the characters involved, did not occur and do not exist.

Published by
Myst and Lace Publishers, Inc.
1386 Fair Hill Lane
Elkton, Maryland 21921

Printed in the U.S.A.
in Baltimore, Maryland
by Victor Graphics

Typography, Layout and Cover Design
by Kathleen Okonowicz

Dedication

With fond memories of St. Hedwig's School,
where adventures in learning and imagination began.

Ed Okonowicz

Acknowledgments

The author and designer appreciate the assistance of those
who have played an important role in this project.

This book would not have been possible
without the excellent proofreading and
very helpful criticism and suggestions of:

John Brennan, Barbara Burgoon,
Theresa Okonowicz DeRose, Marianna Dyal,
Sue Moncure, Theresa R. Okonowicz and Ted Stegura.

Also available from Myst and Lace Publishers, Inc.

Pulling Back the Curtain
Opening the Door
Welcome Inn
In the Vestibule
Presence in the Parlor
Crying in the Kitchen
Up the Back Stairway
Horror in the Hallway
Phantom in the Bedchamber

Possessed Possessions
Haunted Antiques, Furniture and Collectibles
Possessed Possessions 2
More Haunted Antiques, Furniture and Collectibles

Ghosts
Baltimore Ghosts: History, Mystery Legends and Lore
Annapolis Ghosts: History, Mystery Legends and Lore
Civil War Ghosts at Fort Delaware:
History, Mystery Legends and Lore

Stairway over the Brandywine: A Love Story

Terrifying Tales of the Beaches and Bays
Terrifying Tales 2 of the Beaches and Bays

Treasure Hunting: Seek and You Shall Find

FIRED!

Halloween House

Disappearing Delmarva: Portraits of the Peninsula People

Friends, Neighbors & Folks Down the Road

Matt Zabitka Sports:
60 Years of Headlines and Deadlines

Lighthouses of New Jersey and Delaware
Lighthouses of Maryland and Virginia

GOLD, Frankincense & Myrrh

A tale of love, magic and a miracle or two

Now when Jesus was born in Bethlehem of Judea
in the days of Herod the king, behold, there came wise men
from the east to Jerusalem, saying, "Where is he that is born
King of the Jews? For we have seen his star in the east,
and are come to worship him."
—Matthew, Chapter 2

Prologue

Not a day passed that Joey didn't reflect, at least briefly, on how and why he had arrived at his peculiar position. In the entire world, not one other person, at this very moment, shared his responsibility. No royal king nor powerful president. Not the wealthiest CEO worth billions of dollars. Even the Pope, with his direct line to Heaven, could not handle this job.

But it wasn't a job, Joey thought, correcting himself. The terms *duty* or *calling* were more accurate. Like the military advertisement used to say: "It's not just a job; it's an adventure." In this case, his once-simple existence had been transformed into a never-ending, 'round-the-clock devotion, which could only be handled by Joey Novak—a 21st century version of Everyman.

Thousands of times his swirling mind had reviewed the series of circumstances that had delivered him to his bizarre place in history. There was the front porch conversation with his former neighbor, who had arranged for his son JJ to join the local baseball team. Then there was Joey's wife, Janice, and her obsession with collecting yard sale junk. Also prominent was his sudden layoff at the fire department, and his argument with the loudmouth after JJ's midget league ball game. Those four incidents, Joey had long ago decided, were the major turning points that delivered him to his present, ever-vigilant state.

But in truth, his wobbly wheels of fate and fortune probably were heading out of control much earlier, like that Friday the 13th when he and Janice went on their first date, or when his parents met, or the moment he was conceived. Joey's snowball of predetermination could even have started rolling downhill almost a century ago—when his grandparents were deposited at Ellis Island.

Perhaps if they had taken different ships, or if one of their horse carts had broken down on the plains of Eastern Europe while on their journey to America. Maybe then Joey wouldn't be where he is today.

But would any historical deviation have affected what he truly believed was a predestined plan, mapped out by fate?

Probably not, he decided, always reaching the same conclusion.

Even if the crowded immigrant ships had sunk in the North Atlantic, if his father had been killed in the war or if a trolley had crushed his mother when she was a child crossing the street—Joey Novak knew, in the core of his very aged heart, that he would still be right where he was at that moment . . . seated beside the same dirty saloon window, patiently watching and waiting for his successor to arrive.

But that's the end of our story.

Like all good adventures, it's best that we start at the beginning.

CHAPTER 1
Joey, Janice and 'JJ'

Joey Novak was an ordinary guy—nobody special, just one of the unnoticed masses traveling through life on the way to the Great Beyond. He was honest, put in a full day at work and was happy to sit home and spend time with the family. Appearance-wise he would pass as average—not Brad Pitt or Robert Redford, but not Freddie Kruger either. Joey was, just, well, ordinary in the looks department.

He often told his wife, Janice, "You married me for my body." But his football-playing, touchdown-running physique had given way to the mid-30s, getting-a-bit-overweight and the slightly balding look of an aging Michael Keaton.

"But I still love you, anyway," is what Janice would say, smiling as she rubbed his stomach or flipped up the hair on the back of his neck.

Janice was what Joey described as "a looker," with great legs, a trim, shapely figure and a stunning face framed by long dark hair. She looked a lot like Natalie Wood or Marisa Tomei. She and Joey had met in elementary school, gone steady through high school and were destined to marry, settle down and raise a family. And that's exactly what they did.

The young couple lived in a small brick rancher in a modest suburb of Philadelphia. In appearance, cost and status the neighborhood was much closer to blue-collar middle class than the city's swanky Main Line mansions where Grace Kelly was raised. But the Novak's area was peaceful, quiet and safe. The small lawns were neat and clean, and the residents up and down the tree-lined streets were friendly.

"It's like a city block in the suburbs," Janice had told her mother when the young couple decided to move out of the inner city where they had been raised.

Joey's idea of a good time was watching the Eagles or the Phillies on the tube, listening to the callers on WIP sports talk radio and playing poker a few times a month with a handful of close friends. He was realistic and didn't expect too much from life, for he knew that fate randomly dished out good luck and bad breaks. He had gotten more of his share of the latter and was hoping, but not believing, that a few better deals eventually would come his way. In the meantime, Joey took life one day at a time.

"All the workin' man needs is a cold beer, air conditioning and a color TV," was one of Joey's favorite sayings, and one he had told to his son over and over again. But his 9-year-old namesake would never hear the proverb, since Joey Junior, or JJ, as he came to be called, was deaf. Hearing impaired was the current acceptable terminology.

The boy had been born that way, and no amount of medical magic or spiritual intercession would change the youngster's physical infirmity. So while other neighborhood kids played on sports teams, performed in musicals or carried an instrument in the marching band, JJ was sent away to a deaf institute in Pittsburgh, where he played on teams and performed in school plays—using sign language as opposed to speaking the dialog.

When he came home for summer and weekend visits, he was dropped back into a hearing world dramatically different from his residential school environment. Eventually, he got used to reacting to flashing fingers and waving hands, and sometimes even shoves and grabs rudely inflicted by those who wanted to attract the "deaf kid's" attention.

Because of his inability to hear, JJ's speech was different than that of people with normal hearing. Therefore, the youngster often noticed puzzled reactions from those with whom he tried to communicate. As a result, JJ spoke as little as possible and, instead, wrote notes onto a small white pad that he carried wherever he went.

Joey Novak knew early in his son's life that he could not always protect or even help his boy. From his front porch, during JJ's summer vacations spent at home, Joey noticed the taunts, and he flinched when he heard insensitive remarks directed toward his son. It hurt even worse when people ignored the young boy, avoiding him as if his deafness was a disease they might catch. Joey also learned to tune out his wife's midnight tears, and the whispered requests she made to God, offering up a daily rosary and a growing list of other manufactured earthly penances in exchange for a medical miracle that he knew would never come.

After a decade of disappointment, the Novaks accepted the reality that JJ's hearing would never improve. But each did so in a different way. Silently, Janice held onto ragged scraps of faith and optimism—all the while knowing each effort to rekindle her hope would only result in cold embers of disappointment.

But Joey swore he would never allow himself to be lured into the fantasy that JJ would ever be like normal youngsters. When his wife's prayers went unanswered, Joey turned his back on the church and the heartless God who appeared deaf to his family's needs.

"It's all a pipe dream," he would tell Janice when he saw the pain in her swollen eyes. This reaction occurred after another group of white-coated specialists gave her bad news, or when the latest promising Internet chat-room information on experimental surgery was debunked.

"Give it up!" he would shout, his anger boiling over when she tried to drag him back into her web of hope that always ended in misery. "That's the only thing your prayers will bring you," Joey snapped, "more tears and pain. Besides, he's a good kid. We're not that bad off. It could be a lot worse. We can deal with this as long as we work together."

But their arguments were the result of a much more serious and frustrating issue—one each parent realized but never dared address. JJ's "problem," as Janice called it, was the reason they would never have another child. Before JJ's birth, they had planned on raising a large family. But Joey didn't want to bring another impaired baby into the world, and Janice felt deficient and responsible for creating a child who had to endure the hardships heaped on him by an insensitive society.

So the young couple existed in a small, neat house that enclosed their sad private world. Most of their days were calm and uneventful, except when Janice periodically experienced severe waves of depression. Each time that occurred, they were reminded that their family's future would exist under an endless horizon of dreary gray clouds, with no real chance of ever enjoying a bright colored rainbow.

But that was all about to change. An out-of-control lightning storm was heading their way.

CHAPTER 2
At the Ballpark

It was late summer, approaching the end of August, when the fight happened. In only a few weeks JJ would be leaving home and heading for the school in Pittsburgh where he lived during most of the nine-month academic year.

Those two weeks during Christmas vacation, and the summer months when he was home, were very special for his parents. Joey saved up his three weeks of vacation to be with his son as much as possible. But there was never enough time.

This year in particular, Joey had enjoyed the hot months with JJ more than any year in the past—thanks to a well-liked neighbor who had a son JJ's age. Mike, who lived three houses up the street, had convinced Joey and Janice to allow JJ to play on the local church summer baseball team.

Joey knew in his heart it was a bad idea, but Janice, with prompting from their son, wore down her husband. They signed up their youngster for the Midget Phillies in the 9-12 age bracket.

The coach knew JJ's situation and promised he would take extra care to make sure things went smoothly. Through the weeknight and weekend practice sessions, JJ was elated to be a part of a neighborhood group. He became friends with kids who lived on the same block, but who had never gotten to know JJ because he went away to school.

During that special summer, JJ smiled and posed for pictures in his new red, pinstriped uniform. Midway into each game he raced to his position in right field, a spot where he would do the least amount of damage to himself and the team. The coach kept his promise, making sure each boy played in a portion of every game, regardless of his skill level.

Joey, while outwardly reserved, was thrilled his son finally had a group of friends. Just as important, however, was seeing his wife's grins and her inward joy, savoring the special moments when her JJ was truly happy. For the first time, the Novaks met new, friendly people at the games and practices. Most satisfying of all was that during his time on that baseball diamond, JJ looked like, and was treated like, everyone else. But that acceptance did not always apply in the stands.

Anyone who has been to a child's baseball game knows two things: First, because youngsters are unskilled there are a large number of pitches thrown, and errors and hapless mistakes are common. These conditions usually extend an after-dinner, seven-inning game into the late hours of the evening, causing restlessness and agitation among the spectators.

Second, many parents think they can run the team better than the coaches, who are dealing with high-energy youngsters in the dugout. And some fathers *know* their kid is the next Babe Ruth or Willie Mays, and are sure the other kids on the team are not as athletically gifted. The combination of these factors causes parents to say stupid things.

Joey worked in Philly as a firefighter. He had 15 years on the job and was well liked and soft spoken. To earn extra money, he bartended at the Welcome Inn, a shot-and-beer hangout in the Fishtown section of the city. The bar was owned by Joey's Uncle Lou, and had been in the Novak family since before Prohibition. Today, it served as a haven for a band of regulars who considered the watering hole their second home.

Because of shift work, a second job and the need to get some shuteye whenever he could, Joey was unable to attend all of JJ's games. But the boy understood, and Joey delighted in hearing his wife describe—in minute detail—JJ's on- and off-the-field exploits, filling Joey in on each hit, catch and humorous error.

But Janice didn't mention everything, particularly the occasional insensitive comments by other spectators about JJ.

It was a Thursday night, about 8 o'clock, when Joey had finished up his day shift at the house and a 5-to-7, happy hour stint at the Inn. Instead of heading straight home as he has planned, Joey raced over to the ballpark, hoping the game was still under way. If so, he figured he could catch the final inning and take Janice and JJ out afterwards for an ice cream treat.

As he approached the stands, he saw Janice sitting at the end of the second row of bleachers. Smiling, she picked her purse off of her blanket and made room for her husband.

"You're just in time," she said, "JJ's the next batter. We're down by one run, bottom of the seventh. We have one man on. Only one out."

"Make that two outs," Joey said, holding her hand as JJ's teammate flied out into center field. "Talk about pressure," Joey sighed, watching his son head excitedly toward home plate.

"Our JJ can win the game," Janice said as she squeezed tightly on her husband's hand. She watched proudly as JJ swung his bat back and forth, warming up as he approached his position near the opposing team's catcher.

"Oh NO!" shouted a voice three rows above the Novaks. "No way, Jose. This kid's a major league LOOOOSER!"

Janice's body flinched at the cruel words. Joey couldn't believe what he was hearing and began to turn around.

"Please, don't look at him," Janice pleaded, her voice a whispered hiss, mirroring her pain and anger.

"Whadaya mean don't . . . ." Joey's voice snapped at her. He was trying to get a look at the source of the insult.

"Look," Janice pointed, forcefully directing Joey to watch their son wait for the arrival of the first pitch.

"High, BALL ONE!" shouted the umpire.

The Phillies cheered along with JJ's coach from the dugout.

"LUCKY BREAK!" shouted the annoying voice. "GET READY FOR A CHOKE!"

Joey began to turn, but Janice again directed his attention to the game. "I think that guy's drunk," he said, getting angrier by the second.

Janice knew her husband rarely became upset. At the firehouse, he was always in control. As a bartender, he patiently listened to other people's problems. As a husband and a parent, he was a role model and wonderful partner. But she also knew that when he did lose composure, the object of his anger would never win if a conflict developed. She had seen it only twice, and while she felt safe with her husband by her side, she was fearful for what damage he was capable of inflicting on anyone who tried to stand up to him.

"STRIKE ONE!" was the call as JJ swung hard at a low pitch and his body spun to the ground.

"I THOUGHT THE KID WAS DEAF, NOT BLIND!!" screamed the voice.

Several spectators told the loudmouth to quiet down, but he was not to be corrected. "It's a free country, isn't it? Shut the hell up, yourself!" he snarled.

Joey began to stand up from his seat as his son prepared for the next pitch. Splitting his attention from the batter's position at home plate and the top of the bleachers, he wanted to get a look at the wise mouth who was insulting his son.

Suddenly, JJ's coach got the team into the game, shouting, "Let's hear some chatter, guys!" And in unison the team began the rhythmic chant of "JJ! JJ! JJ!" as the home team dugout and parents in the stands clapped along.

Janice joined in and clapped her hands as her voice shouted along with the rest, "JJ! JJ! JJ! JJ!"

But the enthusiastic surge of support died abruptly when the umpire called out "STRIKE TWO!"

Through the silence, as harsh as a knife to the heart, Janice and Joey heard, "WHATTHEHELL DID YOU EXPECT? THE KID'S DEAF AS A POST. HE CAN'T HEAR ANY CHEERING! SAVE YOUR BREATH. THIS GAME IS OVER!"

Joey saw the wise guy, a large, overweight, beer-can holding annoyance, with a head like a pale pumpkin. Pulling his arm away from Janice's grasp, he began to move higher into the stands. But the crack of the bat grabbed his attention, and Joey Novak's face beamed with delight and shock as JJ's ball headed toward the outfield, aiming straight for the railing lined with advertising signs. The stands were cheering. People were yelling, "Go! GO! GO!" wishing, commanding the ball to extend beyond the chainlink barrier.

From the right side of the outfield a tall opponent raced toward JJ's hit. With each long stride Janice prayed that the boy in the gray uniform would fall, not reach his target, disappear or be swallowed up. Anything that would stop him from denying JJ his brief moment of glory, his first taste of success.

But gray clouds were more powerful than Janice's rainbow of hope. The visiting team's long-armed outfielder reached out for JJ's ball, leapt into the air and, in a spectacular catch, swallowed the small white sphere into his brown leather glove.

Cries of joy and cheers of hope turned into disappointed moans as the outfielder fell to the ground.

JJ, who was approaching third base, stopped to see the catch.

His coach shouted for the boy to continue running, but JJ couldn't hear. Didn't respond.

"SHIT!" the beer-can man screamed from his perch in the gallery, adding with disgust, "I TOLD YOU THAT KID WAS A LOSER!"

Joey, who had heard enough, ripped his arm away from of his wife's tight grip and started moving up into the stands, heading toward the guy with the big head and bigger mouth. But Janice was shouting hysterically, pointing toward the outfield and yanking wildly with her other hand on Joey's pant cuff.

Annoyed by having his attention pulled in three different directions, Joey didn't realize the game *wasn't* over.

"HE DROPPED THE BALL!!" Janice screamed, as everyone on and off the field zeroed in on the white object rolling slowly across the grassy surface.

"RUN, JJ, RUN!" the coach shouted, waving his arms and attracting the confused young batter's attention. Two-dozen crazed teammates pointed their arms frantically, directing the boy to race toward home.

The stunned outfielder in gray snatched up the ball and threw a rocket toward the infield, where a nervous second baseman missed the pitch and watched the ball roll toward the pitcher's mound.

JJ was ten feet from home place.

The pitcher dove for the ball.

JJ had 7 more feet to reach the bag.

The ball was in the air, only 12 feet from the catcher's mitt.

JJ was racing, only 3 feet to experience unimaginable glory.

The ball was in the catcher's control. He was covering the base, reaching down to tag out the runner.

JJ flew into the air, smashed into the much larger opponent and knocked the catcher off the bag.

Another wave of joyous screams tore through the crowd as the small magic ball, for the second time in minutes, fell loose and rolled onto the brown earth.

The umpire was on top of the action. "SAFE!" was the call.

The Midget Phillies won 7-6.

For the first time in his brief but hurdle-filled life, JJ was a hero. And although he could not hear their shouts of joy, JJ's face beamed as his teammates hoisted their winning slugger onto their shoulders. Janice wiped her tear-filled eyes with her sleeve and pulled her husband closer. "Enjoy this moment," she said, directing Joey's attention toward the wonderful scene occurring at home plate.

And Joey, again controlling his desire to beat the loudmouth jerk into the ground, listened to his more sensible wife and chose the enjoyment of the glory of goodness over the tempting satisfaction of revenge.

A few moments later, as JJ received his final pat on the back from a teammate and a handshake from the coach, the Novak family headed toward Janice's car. JJ was jumping like a baby rabbit, waving his arms and using his hands to tell his parents that it was the "best day in his whole life." As they reached Janice's Chevy, Joey hugged his son and arranged to catch up with them at the ice cream stand.

While walking alone toward the other side of the parking lot, near the now deserted and unlit field, Joey noticed a figure leaning against the shadowed portion of a tree, urinating. It was the pumpkin-headed jerk from the stands.

"Great game, huh, Bud?" Joey said, slowing down his pace.

"Coulda been better," he snapped, slurring his words. "My nephew's team shoulda won. Would have if it wasn't for that little deaf kid. Bastard finally connected with one."

"Yeah," Joey said, knowing he should walk away, but instead giving into the more tempting but dangerous voice coming from his left shoulder that told Joey to stay.

"Never thought that little retard had it in him," the man said, zipping up his pants and walking toward Joey.

The guy stood over six feet tall and weighed nearly 50 pounds more than Joey, but it didn't matter. Working in his family's bar since he was 16 had taught him how to take down much bigger drunks. Joey decided he had heard more than enough, and he had found the proper target upon which to release his raging anger.

"What's your name, Bud?"

The big guy stopped, looked at Joey and asked, "Why?"

"You remind me of somebody. I thought I might know you."

"I go by Mac. Got it, pal?"

"Got it, Mac," Joey said. "I bet they call you Big Mac?"

"Yeah, they do. So what's this all about, asshole? I don't have time for playin' games. Got to head home. So make it fast. You got some kinda problem? Some kinda issue here?"

"Yeah," Joey said, moving swiftly and grabbing Mac by his left ear, and pulling the taller man's body down so their faces were at an even level. "I got a major league issue, Big Mac. I don't like assholes like you referring to my son as a loser or a retard. Get it, Mac?"

Mac initially had grabbed for Joey's shoulders, but Joey used his other hand to apply pressure with his thumb on a sensitive spot on the top of Big Mac's hand.

The pain from Joey's crushing grip on the large man's ear, coupled with the intense pain flaring up from his pressure point, caused the bigger man to fall toward the ground and rest on his knees.

"I want an answer, Big Mac, or I'm gonna rip your ear off and stuff it in your wiseass mouth."

Straining to speak, Mac quickly gave in and snarled, "All right. Yeah."

"*Yeah* isn't gonna do it, Mac," Joey, pushing down harder with his thumb, hissed at his victim. "I need more."

"Whadaya want?" moaned Mac, who was experiencing intense pain.

"Think in terms of an apology, you dumb asshole," Joey suggested, while simultaneously pulling and twisting harder on Mac's left ear.

"Let the hell go. You're ripping my ear off."

"You can carry it home in your pocket if I don't get what I want, real fast," Joey snapped, enjoying the sense of power and the opportunity to take out years of frustration on the obnoxious loudmouth.

"SORRY! I'm sorry. All right? Let me GO! I won't do it again."

Almost disappointed that the big man had given in so quickly, Joey released his hand holding the bright red ear. Then, squeezing more tightly on the man's hand, Joey snarled, "If I ever hear you say one damn word about my son again, I'll be back. But if that happens, I'll cut out your tongue with a knife. Understand, Mac?"

Unable to talk through the pain, Big Mac nodded frantically and opened his eyes only after Joey released his grip.

The humiliated loudmouth was still sitting under the tree, rubbing his hand gently over his bruised ear, as Joey drove away. After he had gotten about a mile from the park, Joey's sense of satisfaction began eroding, and a slight twinge of fear took its place. While the opportunity to release his anger was welcome, his mind quickly started reviewing the possibilities of being charged with assault or having the deranged victim try to get even with his family. As an afterthought, there was a brief moment when he was disappointed with himself for losing control. But that passed quickly.

Something had to be done, Joey told himself. You couldn't let the world be taken over by obnoxious bullies who prey on the weak and innocent.

Chapter 3

Bearer of Bad News

Joey, Janice and JJ had a wonderful evening, eating ice cream, laughing, and reliving the moments of glory of the final inning victory. Joey never mentioned the incident under the tree, and for the remaining few weeks of the season there was no sign at the games of the obnoxious loudmouth who had insulted his son.

But the secret would not remain unknown forever.

The legal-sized letter came with an escort, who explained that the brown envelope was for Joseph Novak, who would have to sign for its receipt. Janice directed the process server to the Welcome Inn, where Joey was just beginning his Wednesday evening shift. Confused and worried, she called her husband, explaining the man was on his way.

Since he had been warned, the legal exchange went off without a problem. Joey guessed correctly that the document had to do with the altercation with Big Mac. What he could not have guessed was the man he had threatened was a downtown lawyer, and that Joey was being sued in civil court for the attack.

There was no threat of criminal prosecution. Big Mac wanted a written apology and $10,000 in civil damages to make the incident go away. Otherwise Julian MacElvery III, Esq. would file a criminal assault charge and have Joey Novak arrested.

After reading the papers, Joey decided he needed privacy and someone to explain where he stood and his options. He went to the bar's old pay phone booth, shut the accordion-style door and pulled out his cell phone. After a few rings, his cousin, Stan, a real estate lawyer, was on the line. Stan took a few notes and promised to have some free legal advice later that evening or first thing the next morning.

The rest of the night passed with no news from the family attorney. Since Joey had not taken any of Janice's numerous calls, his wife was furious by 1 a.m. as he walked through the back kitchen door.

"Where have you been?" she snapped.

Joey shook his head and waved her off with his hand. "Not now, boss. I can't handle the third degree. I've had a rough night."

Enraged at being dismissed after being kept in the dark for five hours, Janice lashed out, shouting, "Who do you think you are, ignoring my calls and now telling me to back off? I have been waiting here, all night, alone, wondering, scared to death, about what's going on. You don't answer my calls. You don't respond to my messages. Now you dismiss me like some nobody! I want to know what that letter is about."

Wearily, Joey answered, "Look, everything will be fine. We'll talk in the morning. Tomorrow. I'm beat, Jan. I gotta get some sleep. I gotta be at the firehouse by six. Please, let it go."

"NO, damnit! It's not just all about you. If there is something you have a problem with, I want to know about it. It affects us, not just you. Tell me, for God's sake. What kind of trouble are you in now?"

The question hung in the air like a beach ball waiting to be hit by a telephone pole—a can't miss, grand slam invitation to knock the sitting target out of the park. And Joey, after a long night of worry and fear about what the future would bring—and angry at himself for his damn stupidity a month earlier, when he should have ignored Big Mac and controlled his emotions—made another mistake and answered his wife with an ugly personal attack.

Turning slowly, his face a tight, evil mask, Joey snarled, "You want to know what's my problem, Jan? Okay, here's your answer. You're my goddamn problem. You and your rosary recitations and prayer vigils and unrealistic, Miss Goody Goody outlook all the time. That's my major problem. You've got this out-of-this-world, hopeful attitude that one day JJ will wake up and be able to hear and speak like everyone else. That's my main problem. Like God really cares about you and me and JJ. God played an evil joke on us and you keep going to Him for help. Forget Him. He's forgotten us."

Janice didn't move. Her face displayed shock and disappointment as her gaze fell toward the floor.

"Then there's your turn-the-other-cheek attitude, like that night in the stands when the damn creep was rippin' on our kid. And you, Miss Nice, kept me from telling the wiseass off. Well, you got your way that night, like you do all the time. But, you see, it backfired. And I got even with the wise mouth, roughed him up in the park on the way home. But I guess now you'll be happy because since I didn't listen to you, the damn lawyer that I beat the hell up is comin' after my ass. Satisfied, Jan? We're bein' sued, and I don't really know what to do, how to handle it, and I don't want to think about it or talk about it right now, especially with you.

"So here's the papers," he said, tossing them across the room onto the floor. "You can read them and then go upstairs and pray to whatever saint this week might answer your begging. As for me, I've had it with you, with life, with Jesus Christ and all those other decision-making bastards that keep dealing us a string of stinking, no-win hands."

Janice was stunned. She said nothing as she knelt on the floor and began reading the legal complaint. Her eyes widened as she discovered the details and looked up at Joey, speechless.

"Don't look so surprised, Jan," he said.

"But you . . ."

"But what?" Joey snapped, "I told the bastard off? So what? The lowlife was making fun of our son, Jan. He was mocking him because he can't hear. He deserved a lot more than I gave him. And you know what? I would do it all over again, and even worse. So spare me the holier-than-thou speech. All right?"

Enraged, Janice snapped. She wasn't about to take the blame for her husband's uncontrollable actions. Jumping up she shouted, "Don't turn this around on me, Joey Novak. You're the one that got us into this. You think you're so smart and so tough. Well, you can get yourself out of this.

"You don't scare me! Your insults hurt, but they won't break me. You're not the only one who feels JJ's pain, who suffers every time he's overlooked or abused. I'm his mother, damnit! I made him. Do you think I don't wonder every single day why I couldn't give us a son who was physically perfect, like all the other children we see? You'll never know what it's like to live with that, Joey. Never."

Joey didn't know what to say. He and his temper had done it again, and he couldn't think of an appropriate response. There was nothing he could do that would heal his wife's hurt. He felt a sense of shame, knowing he had said too much, gone too far. Now it was his turn to stare in silence.

"You're not going to get any sympathy from me, Joey Novak. You better make this thing go away, and do it fast. I don't care if you have to apologize in the middle of Broad Street. Just do it, and do it soon!"

With tears starting to fall down her cheeks, Janice calmly folded the legal document, placed it gently on the kitchen table, turned and walked upstairs to bed.

Speechless, Joey sat in a chair near the window, shaking his head as he saw the upper hallway light go dark and heard the bedroom door close gently and the lock click.

Chapter 4

Above the Garage

Joey knew the room he had built above the garage would come in handy. It was 1:30 in the morning. He was in big trouble, alone, and had no idea how he was going to come up with the money to pay off Big Mac or find the willpower to apologize. The lawyer's demands were unrealistic, since Joey felt no remorse and did not believe he should pay for his actions.

Maybe Stan would have some helpful advice in the morning. But his cousin knew about settlements and property lines, not assaults and lawsuits. A pessimist, Joey was preparing himself for a slew of legal fees and a painful ordeal because of his impulsive actions, which had seemed so right at the time.

Slowly, he walked across his cluttered, garage hideaway—passing by scattered pieces of junk, old collectibles and broken items that should have been thrown away long ago. He was tired and trying to clear off the old couch where he could rest for the remaining few hours before he had to be at work.

But as precious moments ticked by, Joey discovered that his wife had buried the old sofa beneath a landfill of unused Christmas boxes, yard sale rejects and old baby clothes. Enraged at himself and at her unsympathetic attitude, he began throwing wildly whatever he could grab. Clothes flew in one direction, cardboard in another. The floor was covered with multicolored debris. The last item barring his body from flopping onto the frayed cushions was a battered leather and cloth suit-case he remembered telling his wife to throw away years ago.

The full-size, yellow-and-brown, dented bag looked like the ones seen in the grip of refugees, huddled on shadowy train platforms in black-and-white World War II movies. Tired and desperately needing sleep, Joey yanked on the empty suitcase handle and—using it to take out his frustrations against his wife—hurled the fragile box toward the other end of the garage.

That's when he heard the crash, followed by distinct clinks, as several metal objects fell onto the wooden floor.

After turning and walking slowly across the room, Joey knelt and carefully picked up three engraved gold coins, each with matching designs, that had fallen from a small brown pouch. At that moment, Joey knew there would be no sleeping that night. Something told him his life was about to change, but he had no idea how dramatically different it would become.

*   *   *

Joey placed the gold coins on the floor, stacking the three of them neatly beside the small ripped bag. He examined the interior of the suitcase and found the tear in the lining from which they apparently had fallen. Carefully, he placed his fingers in the torn opening and felt a hidden piece of paper.

Cautiously, he pulled the thin white envelope from the darkness of the suitcase, took out a square-shaped letter and turned it over, looking at both sides. There was no address. Only a small gold seal that was affixed to the back. Pulling a penknife from his back pocket, he delicately pried the gold marker away from the paper and released the flap.

Inside was a note, which Joey unfolded and read:

Dear Friend:

A world war is coming and will soon engulf this continent. It will be a global conflict, the likes that has not been seen in all of history, and it is my duty to insure the safety of the golden coins that have been in my possession for these many decades. To keep them safe from the Nazi invaders, I have secreted them away inside this common satchel, hopeful that they will remain undetected until the time arrives for their discovery by you.

Obviously, now the long awaited moment has come, as I have been anticipating your arrival for quite some time.

I know you are reading this and thinking if it may be a hoax. 'Why me?' you are certainly asking. You also are wondering if you should follow these instructions or toss them aside and sell these valuable coins.

But in this instance you have nothing to decide. You have been designated and you will reply to this invitation because you are both curious and, more importantly, because you have been selected. You have no other choice.

As you begin your journey, you are directed, no commanded, to keep everything you will read in this correspondence in the strictest of confidence. It also is critical that you place the three most valuable golden pieces of coinage in a very secure location.

It is imperative that you do not disclose their existence to anyone, not even to your most trusted spouse, children, parents or associates. The valuable coins' origin and unique powers and purpose will be explained to you in good order. However, it is crucial that their discovery remains secret from all. These are most sought after valuables, and it would be catastrophic if they were to fall into the possession of questionable and unprincipled forces.

You are now the Keeper of the Coins, and with this role comes significant responsibility. Your selection has not been initiated by accident, for your role was predetermined decades ago. However, the circumstances, time and place related to your current discovery were unknown, but, nevertheless, an eventual certainty.

As Keeper of the Coins you must follow these instructions to the letter: Within 24 hours bring this document, but not the coinage, to Isadore Bloom. I am awaiting your arrival at 789 Sansom Street, Apartment 3, on the third floor, in Philadelphia, Pennsylvania, United States of America. The building is located in the district of that city that is commonly known as Jewelers' Row.

It would be most convenient that you arrive, alone, between the hours of 6 and 9 p.m. Ring the bell at least four times and you will gain access to my apartment.

Do not bring any person with you.

On this day, this very moment, your life, and that of your family and closest friends, has been changed drastically. But it is all for the better. However, you also have assumed tremendous responsibilities that will be explained to you in full detail at our meeting.

I anticipate your arrival.

Sincerely,

Isadore Bloom

Warsaw, Poland

July, 16, 1939

Slowly, Joey placed the letter back in the envelop, returned the coins to the pouch and sat on the worn and dirt-stained couch. With his hands clasped between his knees, he wondered if he was in the midst of a dream, or having what the psychics call an "out of body experience." But that was impossible. He looked around the room, even pinched his forearm. He wasn't asleep. In fact, there would be no sleeping for the rest of the night.

CHAPTER 5

The First Meeting

The next day, Joey called his Uncle Lou from the firehouse and told him he would not be working the bar that evening. At noon, after several hours of mental gymnastics and attempts at logical thinking, he made the decision to go to Jewelers' Row and meet the mysterious Mr. Bloom. But Joey still was 99 percent certain he was the victim of a ridiculous, but creative, hoax.

There was no way he would have told Janice about the letter. Besides, she still wasn't talking to him and she hadn't been awake when Joey left for work at 5:20 in the morning.

He had considered getting an opinion about the letter from the guys on the shift or his lieutenant. But something about the message, maybe the warnings, made Joey keep the bizarre situation to himself.

Thinking about the strange invitation to Jewelers' Row helped him keep his mind off the lawyer's letter and his argument with Janice. Besides, after work he would already be in the city. So he ate at a nearby diner, drove over to the old section of town, parked his car and walked along the narrow street, looking for 789 Sansom.

It was 6:30 p.m. and hot for late September. The sun was still high enough in the sky that the fronts of the three-story row houses facing west were illuminated, making their door numbers easy to read.

Since before the Civil War the two square inner city blocks offered more jewelry per square foot than any other city in the world.

Jewelers' Row, established in the early 1850s, is considered America's oldest diamond retail district and one of the largest. Hundreds of independent jewelry stores line the brick paved streets with a wide-ranging selection of fine jewelry at greatly discounted prices.

Everybody in Philly knew someone who knew someone who worked or had a contact along Jewelers' Row. And generations of families often patronized the same retail shop.

On this early fall evening, many of the showrooms were still open, waiting for couples to stop by immediately after work. Whether a particular jewelry shop's storefront was outdated or renovated, its windows were accented with images of gleaming diamonds, sparkling and reflecting off of strategically placed lighting. The historic concentration of shops and catchy advertising all were designed to lure passers-by inside the generations-old establishments—where kindly, gray-haired gentlemen always promised the "best of all deals."

Joey watched a dozen young couples race from store to store, each searching for that very special engagement ring. At the same time, older customers, moving at a much slower pace, carried small bags of family heirlooms, no doubt seeking the best prices for sentimental treasures they were forced to liquidate. Whether buying, trading or selling, Jewelers' Row had a merchant that would cater to every customer's needs.

But Joey wasn't there to buy or sell. He was there to discover what kind of game, or bewildering rabbit hole, he had fallen into. Standing directly across from the address where he would meet the mysterious Mister Bloom, the Philly fireman decided that this crazy game was just that—crazy. He knew he should turn around and head for home—just like he was supposed to do that night at the empty ballpark. His time would be better spent looking for a third job, so he could pay off the fat lawyer he had roughed up in the park.

But . . . .

But, he thought: *what was the note all about? And the coins were real. He held them in his hands just a few hours ago. They weren't gold foil pirate candy or fake tokens, like the painted yellow ones used in board games.*

Even though he had been exhausted the prior night, he took special care, placing the golden coins in a clean, dark blue cloth bag that had held his bottle of Crown Royal whiskey. After setting the folded cloth pouch into the bottom of an empty Chock Full o' Nuts coffee can, Joey buried the container holding the coins in his yard, just to the right of the hose rack in the rear of the garage.

Hell, he thought, looking again at the Sansom Street apartment two floors above the diamond dealing storefronts, *What's the worst that could happen? That some serial killer would kidnap me.*

Laughing, he thought that could be a blessing in disguise and end all of his problems. Then Janice and JJ could live off his insurance.

"Okay, Mister Bloom," he whispered to himself, "let's see what your coin keeper game is all about," and Joey stepped off the curb, heading directly toward the tall row house that had just fallen under the darkened shadow of a passing cloud.

CHAPTER 6

Knock, Knock, Knock

Joey stood in front of a weathered brown, wooden entrance door located in an alcove beside the storefront window of Jerry Lublin's Diamond Mine. Retail businesses occupied the street and basement levels of the building.

Still embarrassed at having come this far, Joey shook off the feelings of stupidity and hesitation. He located the round white button beside the number "3," and reluctantly pressed twice on the bell. In truth, he was hoping there would be no response. Then his current, major league problem would be over. Sure, there were other issues waiting in line for his attention, but at least this mini-treasure hunt could be put to rest.

The situation was not going to be resolved that easily. Within five seconds he leaned on the bell two more times and heard the click of a switch, granting him access to the building. Frowning, he pressed on the latch, pushed against the door and entered the narrow hall. He walked slowly through a dimly lit foyer and headed to a stairway, located to the right of the front door.

Joey took the steps with a sense of uncertainty, heading up toward the third floor apartment where he was supposedly expected. But he couldn't get the thought out of his mind that he would not find anyone there. After all, the mysterious and clairvoyant Isadore Bloom had written the message almost 70 years ago.

Who am I kidding? Joey asked himself, embarrassed that he had let the crazy game pull him this far. *I'm walking up the stairs, alone, and nobody else in the world knows where the hell I am. And when I get to the top, I'm going to ask whatever stranger that opens the door for a man I never met, based on an ancient letter stuffed in a Goodwill Store suitcase that I threw across the room. Oh, yeah, and don't forget the best part, it was holding three special gold coins that I'm not supposed to tell anybody about. I feel like one of those goofy shepherd kids with those stupid hats and vests in a Grimm's fairy tale.*

He stopped on the stairs, thought of turning back. Then he paused, looked over his shoulder, shook his head and muttered, *Hell, I'm here now. Might as well get this part of the mess over with.* Resuming a slow, foot-dragging pace, he reached the second-floor landing.

The building owner must have spent all his money on his storefront, because the higher Joey climbed, the darker and more dismal the building became. Chipped paint, stained ceilings, broken tiles and rubbish resting in corners indicated regular maintenance was a low priority. Obviously, visitors rarely experienced this earthy side of Lublin's glitzy Diamond Mine.

There was some activity down the hall. Joey heard the sounds of typing, on really old typewriters, as opposed to the plastic clicking of computer keyboards. Phones were ringing and voices were answering—talking about orders, appointments, deliveries and overdue payments.

Probably some offices, with bookkeepers and storage for the Diamond Mine downstairs, Joey figured. *Hell, what a crummy place to spend your workday,* he thought. But that wasn't his problem. He was expected on the next floor, so he stepped to the right, placed his hand on the worn, wooden banister and began the final leg of his climb.

When he arrived at the third floor, the hallway was nearly pitch black. He had been in old buildings as part of his job. Most of them at least had a small 10-watt light bulb offering a meager amount of illumination, but this place was ridiculous.

Squinting his eyes and trying to adjust his night vision, Joey felt with his hands along the wall for a light switch that might activate an overhead lamp. He was looking for anything that would help him see where he was heading and be better prepared if some crazed creature was lurking in the purple shadows.

This is nuts, Joey told himself, as again he started to turn around and head for the stairs that would lead him out of the building and onto the safety of the street.

But an inner voice convinced Joey that it would be ridiculous to quit at this point. To which he replied aloud, "This is freakin' insane, I'm going to fall into a shaft and end up in some cave or laundry chute."

With his eyes finally adjusted to the darkness, Joey made out the shape of a single door. The tall, arched entrance was located in the center of the far hall. There was no apartment number, but since it was the only door on the entire floor, Joey figured it must be #3. When he couldn't locate a bell or knocker, he rapped his clasped hand against the thick ornate glass in the center of the door.

He waited 15 seconds. No answer. *One more time,* he told himself, and knocked again, slightly harder than the first try.

Again, no answer. *Well, third time's the charm*, he thought. *Okay, Mister Bloom, this is your last shot and then it's say-o-nar-a and Joey Novak is history. And your three precious gold pieces are heading to the nearest coin dealer first thing this weekend. Then it's off to the slots in Atlantic City with my little, new-found, golden stash.*

This time Joey used the side of his fist, attacking the door like there was an injured victim inside. "HEY!" he shouted, letting loose some of his frustration and nervousness, "ANYBODY IN THERE? YO! ISADORE! YOU INSIDE? YOU TAKIN' VISITORS TODAY, OR WHAT? HURRY UP. I AIN'T GOT ALL YEAR!"

Again, there was no response, and a feeling of relief rushed through Joey's body. There was no need to wonder any longer. The letter was a hoax. The coins were counterfeit, and his very real and annoyed wife was waiting for him and would demand answers to questions he couldn't answer. Also in line were the lawyer he attacked, Joey's dead-end life and the bills and special needs associated with his son.

So Joey slowly began to turn away from the empty apartment, convinced his pessimistic, glass-is-half-empty attitude had once again paid off, prepared him well to deal with his latest letdown. He had taken only a half-dozen steps toward the stairway when he heard a creaking sound. It was loud, as if a sealed wooden casket was being pried apart or an old door with rusted hinges was being forced open after decades of neglect.

Joey stopped and ever so carefully turned to glance over his right shoulder, to look back at the door he had attacked so viciously. But the scene was no longer dark. There was a blinding rectangle of light coming from the inside of Apartment 3, seeping out around a small, dark figured silhouette.

"Isadore Bloom?" Joey asked, his voice a bit shaky as he stared at the short, thin, older gentleman dressed in a formal black suit, complete with vest, white shirt and crisp red bowtie.

"It is I," the image replied in a thin, fragile voice that seemed friendly, but also telegraphed a note of impatience. "You're welcome to enter, Mister Novak, but I dearly hope you will be more delicate with my furnishings than you have been with my front door."

"I'm, I'm, so . . . sorry," Joey stuttered, a bit overwhelmed by the rather petite man and the fact that he really was there, standing right in front of him. "I didn't expect . . ."

"I know," Isadore said, finishing Joey's thoughts," . . . that anyone would be here or that I existed. Well, I do, Mister Novak. May I call you Joey? You can call me Izzy. All right?"

"Fi. . . Fi . . Fine."

"Do you have a stuttering problem or speech impediment, Joey?" Izzy asked, as he waved his hand, indicating the visitor should enter the apartment.

Joey was having a hard time concentrating. He was searching the interior of the tidy room just beyond the doorway with his eyes, while his brain was trying to accept the existence of Izzy and understand the dreamlike circumstances that he was entering into.

"Do you?"

"Do I what?" Joey snapped, turning his head to stare down at the frail, short man closing the apartment entrance.

"Have a speech impediment? Of course, it is no problem and it surely will not affect your ability to carry out your charge. I would surmise that it is temporary, most probably due to your nervousness and uncertainty regarding the present and, to you, rather odd situation. As is to be expected, you seem a bit confused," Izzy said, and then he took off with a brisk step toward a spacious parlor illuminated by large windows that faced the setting sun. "Please, have a seat, Joey." Izzy directed his guest toward a grand, white, wingback chair decorated with blue flowered designs.

"I don't know what to say," Joey said, carefully lowering his body into the appointed seat.

"You don't really have to say very much tonight," Izzy said in an instructional tone. "Your main responsibilities are to listen and to accept the situation, since there is no other option. You see, you found the coins and you are now their Keeper. Just as I, too, once was the occupant of that very important position. And, my dear young man, I have been waiting a very, very long time for you to arrive. I have things to do, places to go. A lot of wasted years to make up for.

"I am so glad you finally threw that old satchel across the room, broke open the compartment and found my note. But," Izzy paused, "I'm getting ahead of myself and you must have a hundred questions."

A leprechaun. That's it, Joey thought, *This little twit reminds me of a freakin' leprechaun. And he's strutting around here ordering me like I'm a trained seal or something. Why, I'd like to grab him by the . . .*

"No," Izzy remarked sternly, as he placed a bottle of beer and a plate of cheese, crackers and pepperoni in front of Joey, "I am not a

Jewish leprechaun, and I do not think it wise for you to resort to force. After all, you have enough problems in that area already. And that altercation in the park is *another* issue I will have to resolve before I can leave town, thanks to you." Izzy shook his tiny head, "They told me this was going to be such an easy job, such an enjoyable task. And here I am, well beyond a hundred years later, still trying to get loose from the onerous responsibilities of this position. Well, anyway," he said, waving his hand, "let's get started."

Joey was beyond stunned. The little nutcake was finishing Joey's sentences, as if he were reading his mind. Somehow Izzy knew about the suitcase and the assault on the lawyer. He must have been having Joey followed by a private eye.

"Nonsense," Izzy said, taking a sip of his bottled beer, "why should I pay for something I am able to do myself. I know about you because it has been my responsibility to know all about you, and Janice and JJ and Uncle Lou your boss at the Welcome Inn, and your deceased parents and your fire station coworkers.

"Joey, Joey." Izzy paused and then spoke in a disappointed tone, "I know more about your past and your future than you will ever imagine. And, to tell you the truth, I want out of this position I have been stuck in for so long. And you, dear boy, are my ticket. But before we begin I want to thank you from the bottom of my heart for doing this."

"For doing WHAT?" Joey snapped. "I don't know what the hell is going on. I don't know if this is a dream or I'm drunk or aliens have beamed me up and I'm stuck in a UFO mother ship. I'm confused, scared and frustrated. And listen, Izzy, or Ozzie, or whatever the hell your name is, I want some answers, and I want them now."

"You like beer, don't you, Joey?"

Joey didn't respond. He was annoyed that the little creep was ignoring the questions.

"I know you like beer, Joey. Look, I even have your favorite brand. Yuengling Black and Tan, Right? Drink up. Have a snack, some cheese. Then we'll talk, and I will tell you everything you want to know. And, believe me, when I am done you will be very relaxed, pleased and quite energized about your exciting future."

Joey looked at Izzy, shrugged his shoulders, picked up the bottle and tipped the top toward his host. "I'll have the beer for starters. Then I want to ask a few questions, probably a lot of questions."

Smiling, Izzy replied, "We have all the time in this world, Joey. All the time in this world."

CHAPTER 7
Questions, Questions

Izzy stood by the window overlooking Sansom Street. Pointing down toward the slow moving traffic, he motioned Joey over to share the view and to focus on the mass of humanity passing along the crowded street below.

"What do you see, Joey?"

"Where?" the fireman snapped, clearly not understanding the question.

"Just tell me everything you see," Izzy urged, tipping the top of the long neck of his brown bottle toward the southern horizon of the city.

"Is this some kinda test or what?"

The smaller man shook his head, trying to assure his guest that it was not a trick question. "Please, Joey, trust me. It's simply a conversation starter, a method for us to begin our dialog. For the third time, please tell me what do you see?"

Taking a sip of his beer, Joey paused a few moments to observe the early evening city scene. The silent moment seemed to drag on while he allowed his mind to wander, to let his thoughts catch up with what he saw on the street below.

In a voice that was much calmer than it should have been in such a strange situation, he replied, "I see confused people, like that couple over there, him in the black jacket and her in the white business suit. She's excited and wants the wedding more than anything, but if you look at the way he's walking, you can tell he's not as eager. Maybe he's being rushed into a commitment. Maybe he's got another girlfriend on the side and he hasn't chosen which one he wants. Or maybe he's just a poor, workin' schmuck who's low on cash. And, of course, in that case he's afraid to disappoint Daddy's Little Girl, who's probably had everything she wants in life. So it could be this guy, he's in love, but he's also really scared of going into hock up to his eyeballs just to impress her with a big ring that he thinks, to her, wouldn't be big enough."

Izzy didn't comment, waited for Joey to fill in the silence.

"Then over there," the younger man continued, "near Sol's Diamonds, there's the poor slob by his cab, leaning against the fender, waiting for whoever's going to come out of wherever. And tonight he needs a decent tip, 'cause he's got bills and payments up the wazoo. Now what he really wants, what he's praying for, is that he makes it home tonight when his shift is over and doesn't get robbed or shot or get into an accident that will suck up every cent he's made the last week on fares and slim tips." Joey stopped, turned to his host and asked, "so, you want some more of my take on life in the City of Brotherly Love, Mr. Izzy Bloom?"

Impressed at Joey's insight, his host smiled, looked at the younger man and replied, "Yes. Only one more observation. Tell me about the couple that will be coming around the corner, right up there," Izzy pointed to the north, "in the next few seconds. Counting down, 4 . . . . 3 . . . 2 . . . 1. There they are, hand in hand. He's in a dark blue zipper jacket, with some sort of team or club name across the back, and she's wearing a pale green short dress."

Laughing, Joey joked, "Well, the wind's blowing pretty good, showing off her great set of legs."

"So tell me about them, Joey. What's their story?"

"All right, Izzy. The guy's a workin' stiff, probably still head over heels about the girl."

"How do you know?"

" 'Cause of the way he's holdin' her real tight around the waist. You only do that when you're crazy in love. That doesn't happen when time passes. I mean, you're still in love, but your brain isn't fried, isn't off-the-charts out of control and rolling you around like a spinning top. That other guy earlier, with the rich girl, he wasn't gaga to the moon like this guy down here is."

"And what about her, Joey, the girl in the pale green dress?" Izzy asked, seeking more insight from his new apprentice.

"She's probably from his neighborhood, works in a deli or a hairdresser's. She just loves the guy and doesn't care if he gets her a fake diamond chip or a gold cigar band. All she wants is to get married, have a buncha kids and live happily ever after. These two, they know they'll never get rich, probably never come back to Sansom Street again, in their whole lives. But the ring, getting any kinda ring is important to both of them. But he wants it to be real nice and big—as big as he can afford. This girl, in the green dress, she'll take anything and be happy and treasure it. She'll even take special care of the blue velvet box, tuck it away in her hope chest. Then she'll pull it out years later, even though it's empty, when she's home all alone. 'Cause it will always be a reminder of this special moment that they had together. Anybody can tell that just by watchin' them, even from way up here."

As Joey was talking he had turned to face Izzy. When he had finished speaking, he looked down at the street below and saw they were walking into Cohen's Gemstones and Heirlooms.

"Hey, that's the same store me and Janice went to when we came down here and boug . . . . "

The realization hit Joey like a brick crashing against his chest. It was he and his wife walking again, at that very moment, into the store in the very same way they had done 16 years earlier. And for a long period of silence, Joey stared, looking down at the joy that had been there at that moment. The carefree, hopeful young couple so much in love, looking forward to a future together until the end of time. No arguments, no frustrations . . . .

"No stacks of bills," Izzy interrupted, "no deaf child, no lawsuits and two jobs and lack of communication and moments of frustration. Yes," Izzy paused and said softly, "all that would come later. But on that day, Joey, you and Janice knew, you knew and believed that you could make a difference together and be happy, oh so very happy."

Joey was in shock, unable to speak.

Izzy continued, "And then life attacked, and things changed. Oh, yes, you are both still in love. But love and life oftentimes don't relate, or don't seem compatible. Sometimes love isn't enough to handle what the world dishes out. But everyone knows that, not just you and Janice. Anyone who has lived learns to expect an endless string of curve balls. Right, Joey?"

The young couple had disappeared into Cohen's store. Joey stared intently, moving from one side of Izzy's apartment window to the other, trying to spot them through the store's large glass picture window.

"They won't be coming out tonight, Joey," Izzy said. "It will do you no good to keep looking. Come, please, take a seat and I'll try to explain all of this."

Joey stayed at the window. "How did you do that?" he demanded. "Was it with some kinda new camera? How much did those actors cost ya?"

"They weren't actors, Joey. They were real. They were you and your wife, appearing again for your benefit to make a point." Izzy was standing near his confused guest. "Look, Joey," Izzy said, placing his delicate hand on the younger man's shoulder, "we need to talk about all this, and it will take a lot of time. I'll need probably two or three days to explain what has happened and to teach you everything you'll need to know before I go away."

"Two or three days!" Joey shouted, moving two steps back from his host. "I took off from work tonight. I gotta get home in an hour, two tops. My shift starts tomorrow at 6 at the house. Look, Izzy. I don't know what's going on here."

"I can deal with the time issue, Joey. You have to keep an open mind, that's all I ask. All right?"

"Whadaya mean, deal with the *time issue*. I told you, all you got's an hour, tops, so start explaining real fast."

"Fine," said Izzy, snapping his finger, "but as you'll see, an hour can mean many things, depending upon who controls the time. Look down there."

Joey saw that the traffic on Sansom Street wasn't moving. "There must be a jam up to the north, near Broad Street," he said.

"What about the people, Joey?"

Joey gasped when he realized they, too, had stopped walking. All of them were frozen in place, like small toy figures arranged on a Plasticville train platform.

"They're not moving, are they?" Izzy asked.

"No," Joey said, his voice now only a slight whisper. "No. They look stiff, like they're captured in a picture."

"And that's where they will stay until we are done. Do you understand?"

Joey didn't respond. He was looking down at his watch, noticing that the sweeping second hand wasn't moving. He tapped his finger several times against the face of the timepiece, but the thin third hand refused to advance. Impatient, he hit the glass cover three times with the heel of his hand—but it still didn't respond.

"I asked, *Do you understand*?" Izzy pressed him.

Jumping a step back from the small man, Joey felt lightheaded. He tried to catch his breath. He looked again at the motionless street scene "Sweet Jesus in heaven, I don't know what the hell is going on here, but I want out. Right now! Get me the hell outta here or I'm gonna . . . ."

"What, Joey, call the police?" Izzy picked up the phone. "The dial tone is dead. It doesn't work. Nothing works and nothing will work until we are done with our sessions. So the sooner you pull yourself together and sit down and we get started, then the sooner this ordeal will be over. Think of our time together as a painful operation. You must go through it to save your life, but you don't want to experience nor remember the agonizing, but very necessary, life-changing process."

"Right," Joey said, his hands shaking slightly as he mumbled to himself and took his seat. Instinctively, he grabbed a beer, which he held tightly in both hands, treating it like a child's security blanket.

"Now you may not want to hear all this, but, as I said earlier, you have been selected. You will do what you are told, and you will do it well, or I will leave this whole world frozen in time and you will wander around alone until the day that you die a very lonely and painful death."

Joey didn't respond. He continued staring at his watch, tapping at the sweep hand, wishing for the thin metal stem to move. But like the street and city and world at that moment, he was at Izzy's mercy.

Chapter 8
All About Gold

"What do you know about gold, Joey? Anything?" The sound of Izzy's voice ended in a large question mark that was aimed at the center of Joey's aching forehead.

Working on the end of his third bottle of Black and Tan in about thirty minutes, Joey had begun to settle down and, at least to some degree, seemed to accept his unusual situation. As a result, his response was fairly coherent. "Most valuable substance in the world," he said, initially speaking softly and cautiously. "It's associated with bigtime wealth. Doesn't rust like tin or steel or other metals. Is found as dust, nuggets and often mixed in with other metals. I think it's supposed to be a bit softer than other ores, and that makes it easier to mold."

"Excellent! Very well done!" Izzy said. "Gold is the world's noble metal. Indestructible. A piece can be melted down and flattened to extremely thin levels. It can be pressed so thin that gold sheets can transmit light. Artists have used gold to decorate statutes. It's been woven into garments and has served as official stamps on royal seals and documents. Graves in ancient Troy, Egypt, Crete, Constantinople have yielded tombs and vessels adorned with gold that the kings and leaders would take to the Afterlife.

"And one more interesting fact, Joey, is that gold does not change over time. It can be buried in the ground, lost in the seas, hidden in a treasure chest, but the Earth's elements cannot degrade it. That's why gold coins found on a beach appear as they were on the day they were minted. On the other hand, silver—another valued, but less precious metal—turns black, and over extended periods it suffers in both quality and appearance—unlike gold."

When Izzy stopped talking and remained silent, Joey figured the little man was waiting for a response. Resigned to his fate, the firefighter decided if he showed some interest it might speed things up and help bring his extended nightmare to an end. "And I'm here because I've found some gold?" Joey asked, trying to sound sincere.

"Correction, my young friend. You have not found *some* gold. You have discovered *the* gold. The world's most precious and most sought after pieces of long lost *golden* treasure."

When Joey did not react, Izzy tossed out a question. "What, Joey, would you consider to be the most valuable gold pieces in the history of recorded time?"

"Hell, Izzy, I don't know. Whadaya mean, 'recorded time'?"

"The history of the world as we know it, Joey. Use that as your guideline."

Thinking for about ten seconds, Joey tossed out a reply. "How about the golden calf from the party the Jews had when Moses went up to the mountain?"

"Not bad," Izzy said, impressed with Joey's historical knowledge and reasoning. "An interesting reply, but incorrect. Please try again."

"How about a brick of gold from Fort Knox, where Oddjob and James Bond had that fight in *Goldfinger*?"

Clearly disappointed, Izzy shook his head and added, "Joey, we are discussing matters on a much higher level here. No movie answers, please. Now, try another. And, I prefer that you be careful to remember that we call the bars ingots, not bricks."

Frustrated, Joey let out a heavy sigh. He wasn't interested in a metallurgical history lesson. But he was eager for a multitude of answers concerning the crazy situation and how it would affect him and his family. Losing his patience, he snapped at his host. "Hell. I don't know. Maybe ingots or coins from the *Nina, Pinta* and *Santa Maria*. Or how about gold from the California Gold Rush? Or maybe the treasure from the Lost Dutchman Mine, or the hidden treasure of the Confederacy, or Humphrey Bogart's *Treasure of Sierra Madre*. Then there's Blackbeard's shipwreck treasure that's supposed to be somewhere in Marcus Hook, down near the oil refineries, only about 10 miles south of here."

"Think in threes, Joey," urged Izzy. "If you think in three's, what we are talking about should become obvious."

"Look, Izzy, it's getting late. I wanna take my broken watch downstairs to one of the jewelers before I head home. Can we wrap up this science and history torture lesson soon?"

"THREE'S!" Izzy demanded, folding his stick-like arms across his narrow chest.

"Damn!" Joey snapped. "The three pigs. Three blind mice. The Three Stooges. Three peas in a pod."

"TWO peas in a pod, Joey," Izzy corrected him. "Go on. I think you're getting close."

"*Three's Company*. Three strikes and you're out. *Three Coins in a Fountain*. That's about it."

"Oh, I think you can come up with a few more. Think Christmas, Joey. Christmas."

"Great. It's freakin' September and you wanna talk about Christmas. Fine! Santa's three flyin' reindeer. Three French hens. Maybe there were three lonely shepherds. Wait! I got it. THREE GOLDEN RINGS!"

Again shaking his head, Izzy reminded his new student, "There were FIVE golden rings! Think *THREE*, Joey."

"Hell, the only thing left is the Three Freakin' Kings. But they got to Christmas about two weeks late. On January 6. And delivered their presents. Gold . . . ."

Joey paused in mid sentence. His body froze and he held his breath, apparently afraid to utter aloud the amazing truth that his mind had just realized.

Smiling, Izzy completed the sentence, "*Gold* . . . frankincense and myrrh. And you, Joey, have in your possession the actual gold that was presented to the Christ Child soon after His birth."

"Jesus Christ!" Joey said, slapping a hand against his forehead as he fell back against the oversized chair and let out a deep sigh.

"Yes, Joey," agreed Izzy, smiling, "that is what *He* is called. Now can we get down to business?"

CHAPTER 9

Getting Down to Business

It was good that Izzy was able to break the steady flow of time, for he and his apprentice discussed the quite unusual situation for nearly 24 hours in normal, everyday time as it related to earthly mortals. But in the magical world of these two Keepers of the Coins, there were no frames of reference, no distractions, nothing to pull them away from the detailed explanations of the blessed gold coins' journey and Joey's new and awesome responsibilities.

This is not to assume, however, that the transfer of knowledge went smoothly. Initially, significant time was consumed convincing Joey that he was no longer a part of the general mass of humanity. Izzy tried to be gentle at first, explaining to his young successor he was now in control of significant "assets" that he must use to better the conditions of his fellow man.

After repeated efforts using a rather delicate vocabulary, Izzy realized that blunt language and dramatic examples were necessary to make Joey "see the light" so to speak.

"Whadaya mean 'assets' and 'bettering my fellow man?' " Joey snapped, unable to comprehend the abilities and responsibilities that were now his.

"It's all about power, Joey," a frustrated Izzy replied. "Why can't you understand that you now have the ability to change things, to have a positive influence on those in need?"

"Are we talking magic?"

Slapping his palms against his knees, Izzy jumped up from his chair and stomped to the window. Turning away from the younger man, Izzy inhaled deeply, raised his eyes toward the sky and said, "Of the billions of people in the world, of the 300 million in the United States, of the 12 million in the Commonwealth of Pennsylvania, and of the several hundreds of thousands within my present line of sight in the City of Brotherly Love, how did it occur that this reluctant bartender, with a limited imagination, had to be the individual to discover the gold?

"Why couldn't it have been a lonely nun, a pious rabbi, a homeless soul more receptive to reason or a young maiden who would welcome with excitement the gifts and ability to change the world? Is this my retribution for losing track of my satchel? Is this my punishment?" Then turning toward his student, Izzy asked, "Are you my Hell on Earth, Joey? Is that what you are, a final test with no answer sheet?"

Joey didn't answer. He seemed to enjoy using long silences to frustrate Izzy.

"Why did they have to send me someone with a mind closed tighter than a . . . . Oh, I simply don't understand." Izzy waved a disgusted hand toward the heavens and sighed.

Joey, who had endured the lengthy critical diatribe, was insulted. Slowly, the fireman stood up and said, "Look, Mr. Isadore Bloom. I did not ask to be directed here. I was invited. I am trying to understand what the hell is going on, but excuse me if I find it difficult to believe that I am being given the *assets* to *change people's lives*. To me this all sounds like a school play—like the Salem witch trials or the *Blair Witch Project*—filled with a lot of hocus pocus, mumbo jumbo, and to me that spells M-A-G-I-C!"

A red flash of anger arose in Izzy's eyes. He was irritated that Joey had not been able to comprehend the seriousness of the moment. Abruptly, Izzy pointed his finger at Joey and snapped. "We are stuck with each other, and it is my job to convince you of your responsibilities. I have demonstrated to you some of our powers. I have stopped time. I have made you and your wife reappear and reenact the best moments of your life. I have sat and explained, quite patiently, this serious situation. It is acutely obvious to me that you have not been listening. You have refused to open your soul and mind to the current and future state of affairs."

Izzy's small body began to tremble. His tiny face was the color of a ripe tomato. "I have tried to complete my mission in a positive fashion, but now—because you have forced me—I will do what I should have done the moment you walked through the door."

When Izzy was finished talking, he took a few moments to gather his composure and forced a weak smile. Pointing directly at Joey, Izzy began twirling his right index finger in a circular motion. The tip of the older man's slowly swirling digit was pointed toward the ceiling, and within seconds that's precisely where Joey was headed.

As his feet left the ground, Joey thought he had stumbled, that his legs had fallen asleep. But as he looked at the floor below, and at the distance that was increasing between his body and the large rectangle of brown and red carpeting, he began to scream.

Izzy heard the pleas, but he returned to his chair, picked up the newspaper and began to read. "No one else can hear you," Izzy muttered softly to himself.

Joey shouted louder. He was hovering like a slow-moving human helicopter blade, about two feet below the ceiling. His spider-like body was rotating in a clockwise direction, his face and chest facing below. He was an awkward puppet held by invisible strings. But there were no wires or lines supporting his floating body, and Joey knew he needed to get back into Izzy's good graces in order to end the human windmill torture.

"I hear you. You don't have to scream," Izzy said in a calm, soft voice, turning to the second page of the sports section.

Joey's body had reached the ceiling, and an irregular thumping sound began as his shoulders, heels and head connected intermittently with the solid surface above.

"ENOUGH! PLEASE, IZZY. STOP!"

Slamming his paper onto the polished mahogany end table, the smaller man walked directly below the levitating body, crooked his finger and lowered Joey to a level three feet below the ceiling, but still about six feet above the floor.

"I will allow you to return to a more practical position if you are able to answer one question, Joey. This will tell me that you are not as utterly obtuse as you appear, that you have a functioning brain and that you have been paying attention to what I have been trying to tell you for all these many tedious hours. Are you ready?"

"Do you think I'm gong to say NO?" Joey replied, his arms waving, his body still moving in a circle, his mind hoping for a soft landing.

"I suggest you lose the attitude," Izzy said. "I can finish the newspaper, go out to a leisurely dinner and return in a few hours."

"NO! SORRY! Please. Yeah! I'm ready."

"Fine," an irritated Izzy looked straight at Joey, who was hovering lower now, only four feet above the carpeting. There was nothing below but the faded oriental run.

Izzy stood off to the side. "Tell me," he said, "what we are talking about. Tell me what you will have the power to perform. Tell me the proper name of the positive deeds that you are being entrusted with conducting. AND IF YOU SAY *MAGIC*, I will leave you up there for a week!"

Joey closed his eyes, trying to concentrate. But he reopened them quickly when he realized the lack of vision was making him sick. As his body continued its steady spin, he looked toward Izzy, locking eyes with the small teacher with each passing rotation.

"Look, Izzy, how many chances do I get?"

"ONE!" Izzy snapped, his voice a snarl. "And the word starts with an M! That's the last hint. I have no more time for games. You have 10 seconds. GO!"

"M and not *magic*," Joey muttered.

"SEVEN!" Izzy called out, taking a few steps back from Joey's twirling torso.

Joey continued to think and mutter softly, still offering no guesses.

"FOUR!"

"Hell, I can't . . ."

"TWO!" Izzy announced, beginning to walk toward the apartment door. He had decided to leave Joey suspended in space to demonstrate the power and to punish him for his lack of attention.

"TIME'S UP. . . ." Izzy called out with his hand on the doorknob, but at the same moment Joey shouted the word "MIRACLE!" Izzy turned abruptly, smiled and began walking back toward the interior of the apartment.

Joey, sporting a satisfied smile, expected a smooth return to the apartment floor, but he was unprepared when his body descended abruptly and smashed onto the threadbare carpet.

Dusting himself off as he rose off the floor, he offered the older man a stiff smile, but silently vowed to get even with Izzy before they parted company.

CHAPTER 10

Rare, Valuable and Coveted

Joey was subjected to a crash course in numismatic knowledge. Izzy explained that a coin's value was determined by its condition, metal content, collector demand and scarcity.

"Two-thousand-year-old Persian drachmas may cost approximately $400, and one-thousand-year-old Chinese currency has sold for only a few dollars. This is because both coins are abundant, since they have been discovered in large quantities and continue to be easily obtainable," Izzy said. "Therefore, just because a coin is very old does not also mean it is very rare and worth a considerable amount of money. Do you understand?"

Joey nodded, "Sure. In my spare time I do a lot of web surfing at the firehouse. A few months ago, I read that a liberty head nickel—that was pressed wrong at the mint and got into circulation with an error on it—went for over a million at an auction."

"True," Izzy said, "because only a handful were minted and, at last count, very few are believed to be in existence. Now, using that fact as our basis, what would you guess to be the value of the coins in your homemade, safety-deposit coffee can buried behind your garage?"

No longer surprised at the extent of Izzy's knowledge about him, Joey replied calmly. "Honestly, I would just be shooting in the dark, but since they are the only three in existence, because gold itself is a valuable metal and, most importantly, because of their significant historical, cultural, religious and mystical value, I would guess about $20 million. Essentially, I would equate them to a single ticket, winning Powerball value. In my humble estimation, that is."

Joey offered a mocking smile and wondered if Izzy had realized the fireman's choice of words and tone were an imitation of his mentor's, at times, stilted and overly precise language.

Impressed that his pupil had considered four critical value components of the coins, and that he had offered a rather good, but still low, estimate of their worth, Izzy congratulated Joey on his analysis.

"But one of the big questions, in my mind," Joey said, "was how did they get here? I don't mean *here*, as in my *house* in *Philly*. I mean through time. How did these small objects make the trip and not get lost or stolen during the last two thousand years?"

Izzy recognized that the dialog was moving to a more substantive level. Joey might not yet be convinced or understand his role, responsibilities and power, but his interest—demonstrated through his speculation and questions—convinced Izzy that the transfer of duties to Joey eventually would work, even though he expected a fair number of bumpy and awkward moments.

The route of the coins and the list of their owners, Izzy explained, were pieced together over time by distinguished historians, archaeologists, astronomers, collectors, artists, financiers and clergy—and even a few astrologers provided details. Some of the information was based on documents located in the secret archives of the Vatican. Other facts surfaced from records in Swiss bank vaults and from government information depositories in the Middle East, Europe and Asia. But, he added, a fair amount of what is now considered fact was based on a considerable amount of speculation, folklore and oral history.

"When the human mind tries to recall what happened decades ago," Izzy said, "or even a few hours earlier, not every memory is vivid or entirely accurate. But those searching for answers about the past must rely on hazy recollections, particularly when they are the only references available."

As real time remained suspended, Izzy leaned back and shared with Joey the tale that he had heard nearly 200 years before, when he initially had become Keeper of the Coins.

"Anyone who has heard the story of Christmas," Izzy said, "knows the tale of the Three Wise Men—Los Reyes Magos. It's said they arrived on January 6, after following a special star in the East that led them to the Christ Child's manger. There they deposited items of tribute, upon which we base the present gift-giving custom.

"This trio of wealthy astronomers—or minor royalty, as some considered them—were from various kingdoms. They may have come from Persia, the Orient, Ethiopia or Arabia, to name a few possible locales. But much depends upon the version of the tale you read and even the original teller's country of origin. They were called Melchior, Balthazar and Gaspar. But over time they would come to be identified with different pronunciations and spellings—for instance, even today the last king's name sometimes is spelled with a C or a K.

"The first king gave gold, in the shape of the coins that you recently discovered. They feature the profile of a crowned king on the obverse and a fire altar, crescent and star on the reverse. The second presented the gift of myrrh, an ointment produced from a valuable gum-like substance with a pleasing aroma. The final king's offering was frankincense, a soft substance considered to be sacred and reserved for burning during special religious ceremonies.

"Countries throughout the world have created customs," Izzy said, "both secular and religious, based on the Three Kings' travels and, in particular, their gift sharing. In many Old World European countries, Christmas present exchanges actually took place on January 6, known as the Feast of the Three Kings or the Epiphany.

"The frankincense and myrrh disappeared rather quickly," Izzy speculated, "probably being used for religious and medicinal purposes by what has been called the Holy Family—Joseph the carpenter, Mary the mother and Jesus the youngster. However, it is believed the coins—the more sturdy and precious gifts—survived after being stored with significant care by Mary, mother of the Holy Child."

Joey listened intently, fascinated with the information he was hearing about what may have occurred after the Kings' visit.

"Upon the death of Jesus," Izzy said, "his mother, Mary, is believed to have moved in with distant relatives for safety. She would have taken the family's few belongings with her. In most of the numerous rites of the Catholic Church, the description of her 'Assumption' into heaven is considered the end of her life on Earth. However," Izzy added, "other religions and classical historians claim she died at a much older age in a distant province under an assumed name for fear of persecution by the Romans. She also did not want to become a focus of attention and detract from the primary mission of her son's disciples—to spread their Lord's word and do good deeds.

"Upon her death, her goods were divided among a few remaining relations—and a dedicated band of highly skilled protectors who had devoted their lives to preserving her safety. A young shepherd, without knowledge of the long-term value of her belongings, somehow gained possession of the coins, and he sold them to a Jewish trader who traveled throughout the Middle East.

"Apparently," Izzy said, "coin collectors, or numismaticists, as they are sometimes called at their special conventions, were active in early world history. One old fellow had an eye for rare and well-fashioned coinage. He recognized the fine workmanship in the three pieces and placed them in a family hideaway, apparently deciding not to use them for daily commerce. It's also believed that he had some inkling of their origin, since his diary and last testament specifically instructed his descendants to take special care with these three particular golden coins.

"One translated document from the Vatican's secret archives states that the merchant instructed: '. . . sell everything you may be compelled to dispose of in times of strife and hunger, but never trade away the three golden coins bearing Herod's crown. For these prized pieces of exchange hold significant supremacy and are allied to a most esteemed prophet. Their origins may be traced to the travels of the wisest of astrologers many years ago who, it's believed, followed the wandering constellation in the East.' "

"Do you really believe these are the coins?" Joey asked.

"You've seen them, held them. I know you examined them carefully. Tell me what you discovered," Izzy replied.

"I didn't know what they were, until seeing you today. But I remember, even though it was very late at night, that I was no longer tired. I just wanted to stay there, sitting on the floor, holding them in my palm and touching them so carefully. It was as if I knew they were special. There was almost a reverence about them."

"What did they look like? Can you describe them?"

Looking up, Joey said, "They're exactly like you just said, a king with a crown on one side and the other had the fire and star. But I had expected them to be old and worn down and jagged around the edges. But these were smooth, sparkling, as if they were made yesterday and just came out of a mint or a package."

Smiling, Izzy said, "That's exactly how they looked when I placed them in the suitcase. And it's probably why they attracted the attention of the Jewish merchant, and later the high church officials, royalty, bankers and soldiers—all who had realized instinctively it was important to keep them safe over time. And then there were the little, average people, nobodies like us, Joey, who realized the coins offered something more important than earthly riches."

Sensing he was making progress, Izzy smiled and continued, "The coins dropped out of notice for some time. They resurfaced at one point, somewhere during the latter years of the Crusades, during the mid-13th century. As the story goes, a serf or servant of one of the knights was rummaging through an overturned wagon, following a battle against the Selnick Turks somewhere in the Holy Land."

Izzy summarized the rest of the story.

The boy came upon a young man and his wife who had been killed in a small village. Their shabby wagon was being ignored as the knights and soldiers seemed more interested in the spoils of war on the adjacent battlefield, eager to plunder what they could from their conquered opponents. Of course, they certainly would return to direct their attention to the village in short order. Knowing this, the peasant rummaged through the recently deceased's belongings, and he came upon a tin box. Not wanting to be found out, he raced into the woods, discovered a stack of papers and a small cloth pouch containing the gold coins. As they were the only currency in the tin, he tossed the other contents aside and stuffed the sparkling booty beneath his shirt.

There was a paper in the pouch and the young man, who was illiterate, decided to await his return to England before he asked anyone to decipher the note and the value of his discovery.

"While that was bad news for him," Izzy said, "it was good news for us."

"Why?"

"Because when he returned to the British Isles he showed the coins to his mother, who marched them and the letter, which she also could not read—to the parish priest. He determined it was written in Aramaic, and could not understand it. As he was of Irish heritage and not a big fan of the British, he contacted a French monsignor. The Irish priest, in secrecy, promptly shipped the valued tokens and document off to Paris for translation. There they remained for a period of time until—and I am summarizing rather quickly here—they somehow came into the hands of a simple but very famous teenage farmer's daughter, who would change the history of France, named . . . ."

"Joan of Arc," Joey blurted out, obviously shocked at the sequence of events in his mentor's fascinating tale. Eager to contribute to the story, Joey added his own comment about Saint Joan, "Who was burned to death at the stake after she beat the invading British at the Battle of Orleans."

"I am impressed, Joey. Very nice, indeed,' Izzy said, complimenting the young man.

Izzy explained that Jeanne d'Arc had been one of the first known Keepers of the Coins, who apparently harnessed their miraculous powers. She shared her belief that the coins were the source of her wisdom and success just before the authorities, who considered her a threat to their power, burned her alive. However, the good reverend who heard the story of the gold during Joan's last testament and confession made arrangements for the coins to arrive in the Vatican—where they were secured.

"It was there, soon after they arrived," Izzy said, "in about the year 1430, that their journey was recorded and their energy was examined and truly appreciated. They remained in safekeeping, and their existence was known only to the Holy Father and his closest aides. It's said they were the strongest tangible link between the Papacy and the Lord Himself, in heaven. Others credit the Kings' Coins, as they sometimes were called, with the source of the Pope's infallibility, allowing him to speak with confidence on matters of Catholic faith and morals. But, Joey, that is for your religion's followers to decide, not mine."

Joey nodded, then interrupted, explaining that he was eager to find out the answers to several questions that had been bothering him for the last few hours.

Izzy was glad to take a brief respite from the chronology and waited for Joey to speak.

"How did you get the coins, and how old are you?" he asked Izzy, knowing that the elf-like man could provide much more important and practical information than the ancient history lesson of the Kings' Coins journey.

Smiling, Izzy thought for a long moment, stared across the small antique table that separated the two men, and said, "I will answer every one of your questions, Joey. And you must believe, despite the lack of logic you will hear in my replies, that everything I am telling you is the complete truth, for Keepers can never deceive one another. So, here is my part of this fascinating saga, a drama and sad comedy in which you, my nervous young colleague, will soon play your own starring role."

Chapter 11

Izzy and the Coins

I was born Isadore Bloomwitz, in a small village in what is now Germany. But at different times it had been conquered by the Swedes, Poles, Tartars, Lithuanians, Hungarians and even the French. As you have guessed, I am Jewish. We had no land or secure country. We were wanderers, the outcasts of Europe, of Northern Africa. No one wanted us, but they all needed us, for our tribes or families were unsurpassed in the skill of making money. We excelled in the area of commerce. Be it managing a store in a village, coordinating shipping and trading fleets across the seas or money changing, loaning or investing. Those in our region seeking such skills would travel to Lublin Street, in my small village that is no more."

"So you were a merchant, a banker?" Joey asked, following along intently.

"No, please, Joey. You flatter me. I was a baker, a simple man with simple needs with common knowledge and no formal education. I could barely read or write. But I could bake such wonderful hearty breads and a variety of light and delicious deserts. Sweet creations so superb that they would melt in your fingers before they reached your mouth. Now this was in the 1830s, when baking involved around-the-clock attention and dedication. We had no modern heating systems or electricity."

Shocked, Joey interjected, "My God. When were you born?"

"In 1812, on January 1, start of the New Year, five days before the celebration that would change my life, the date of the arrival of the kings." Izzy paused, taking a moment to view scenes of his long life. Certainly, he was savoring the memories, but he also was taking care to provide Joey with an accurate picture of the significant experiences and events—for everything he had gone through Joey, in his own way, would soon encounter.

"I was such a wonderful baker that the countess demanded of my father that he allow me to work in their estate on the hill above the village. It was an honor, but also a curse. My family depended on me for help, but the income and prestige of serving the count and countess would bring favor upon my family and my father's small shop. Besides, imagine the son of Abraham Bloomwitz, a Jew, working in the kitchen of the esteemed German countess, Katrina Wassel. It was unheard of at the time. But that is only a minor point in my long journey."

Izzy explained that the woman, who was beautiful and only about five years older then he, took a fancy to him. She saw to it that he learned to read, and Izzy was given a private room in the castle. Eventually, as a result of daily contact and mutual attraction, he became her lover.

"Her husband was off, fighting whatever endless sequence of wars which came along. He loved the thrill of battle and was a mercenary, a very good one, indeed. He was never home and the two of them had a rather modern arrangement—one from which I benefited quite well."

For seven years, until he was 30, Izzy worked for the countess.

"She was a good woman," Izzy said, "always helping the poor, delivering food, sending her workmen to fix the huts of her serfs. She even built a small doctor's office in the village and hired a physician from northern Germany to live there and take care of the people, free of charge. It was just one outward sign of her kind nature.

"But she also had a useful gift; it was the power to heal. At that time, I thought she was simply serving beneath her station as the village midwife, that she somehow had been born with the magical wisdom and skills to mend the sick and to help those in physical and mental distress. I never realized until much later that she was using the power given to her as the Keeper."

Smiling, Izzy paused to reflect upon his first love. Then he looked directly at Joey and continued his tale.

"But then, as has occurred several times in every generation, another purge took place. Sometimes it was based on religion, other times it focused on nationality. This time it was the former. All of the Jews in the region were to be moved to the east, toward the frozen tundra of Russia. A census was held, and my family was scheduled to be shipped away—exiled.

"I visited them three days before they left," he said, softly. "I was going to go with them. But my parents, who were only in their fifties but who looked like they were eighty, made me swear I would stay with the countess. You see, because I worked in the castle, I was exempt, saved. I guess you would say I had been granted a free pass."

Izzy stopped talking. A single tear fell from his eye and traveled down his lined and weathered cheek. "I should have gone with them, but I was young. At that moment I also wanted to stay with my love, and I remained behind. But not for long. Only two weeks later the tax collectors and assessors and other conquering officials arrived. They had come to seek out any remaining Jews and move them out of the region. One saw me working in the castle kitchen. He threatened to expose me as a criminal who had gone against the edict.

"Katrina argued on my behalf, but despite her royal station she was a woman alone, with no husband to protect her interests and authority. They ignored her and promised to return the next morning to take me away. That night she gave me a pouch of money, documents bearing her family crest that would get me across the border into France and a loaf of bread. I remember what she said to me. It's as if I can hear her voice right now, standing in this very room, 'Take this bread of life, my love. It is your future and a guarantee of a very long life. Do not give it away, do not share it. Be sure that you alone eat every crumb.' And she made me promise that I would follow her instructions to the letter. I answered her affirmatively. We embraced. Kissed passionately. Then she gave me a swift horse, waved good-bye and turned away. That was the last time I saw her."

The room was quiet, too quiet, for an uneasy length of time. Finally, Izzy cleared his throat and spoke. "Apparently, she knew her time had come, her end was approaching. She used me to move the Kings' Coins to safety, to put them out of reach of evil forces. And, in that way, I was selected to carry on her work.

"I later heard they came the next day. Killed all of her servants. Impaled her beautiful head on a pike. All because she had allowed me to flee. I never have gotten over the fact that I was the cause of her death. I've often wondered why I was chosen, from all the people in the world, why me? Why was I given the awesome honor and responsibility to serve as a guardian? I guess I'll never know, not in this life."

Izzy arrived safely in France, eventually found the coins, along with a document in a small pouch hidden inside the loaf of bread. Somehow, he decided, the countess' husband must have secured them as a spoil of war, a trophy from one of his battles, or through a contact in the Vatican, who may have smuggled them out of the vault. One could only speculate on their travels before arriving at the countess' castle.

"She must have known about them. She certainly used their goodness to help others. Then, knowing that evil was approaching, rather than have them fall into the wrong hands, she selected me to become her successor.

"Of course," Izzy said, "this all makes sense to me now, as I reflect on the incidents. At the time, I had no idea of the true significance of what had been taking place."

Incapable of understanding what to do with his newfound wealth—and realizing the treasure had more than just monetary value—Izzy visited a rabbi, who had been recommended by a family he had befriended.

"It was as if the wise man had been waiting for me to arrive," Izzy told Joey. "Just as I have been waiting for you. You see," he paused and touched Joey's arm, "in both our cases, I believe there is a greater force directing what we must do."

Shifting back to the story, Izzy said the old wise man explained what valuable and sought after relics Izzy had been given. Most importantly, he instructed Izzy on how to harness their power and use them for good.

For the next hundred years he traveled Europe and Asia, responding to the needs of others—performing simple kindly acts using riches and the coins' power—all the while protecting the valuables that had been entrusted to his keeping.

"In 1939 I was in Poland," Izzy said. "The Nazis were on the march. I had to protect the coins and also move my family to safety. I should have gotten us all out sooner. My wife told me so. I should have listened to her. But, what man ever listened enough to his wife?"

"You were married?" Joey blurted out the question, and was slightly embarrassed afterwards.

"Don't be so surprised," Izzy said. "You're married. Why shouldn't I also have the comfort of a lovely, caring, passionate woman?"

"Of course," Joey said, agreeing. "I just didn't think that you were ever. . . ."

"Just because I am old does not mean I have never loved, Joey. Love is for all ages. Maybe there is not as much fierce passion in later years; but that, my young friend, is when true love shows itself. When it is easier to take things for granted and it is not as easy to be caring or loving. Remember that. But, yes, I have been married. Five times."

"FIVE?"

Izzy smiled, laughed slightly, then stood up and motioned for Joey to follow. The two men walked down a narrow corridor and turned into a small bedroom on the left side of the hall.

"My study," Izzy said, softly. There was sadness in his voice. Flicking on a light, he pointed to a wall completely covered with framed photographs. The pictures—plus older paintings, ambrotypes, pen-and-ink sketches and Polaroids—showed men and women, children and relatives in various stages of life. There were celebrations—birthday and graduation parties, weddings, bar mitzvahs, baby pictures, Halloween costume parties.

"I don't come in here often anymore," Izzy said. His voice was sad and soft. His frail body seemed like it had difficulty remaining upright. "I have outlived them all, and I out loved them all," Izzy said, looking at the photographic pageant on display. "For that is part of our Keepers' curse. We, you and I both, Joey, will most likely outlive so many friends, lovers, even children. And while nothing is certain or guaranteed, like I have done, you will feel your heart ache with the passing of each loved one. Eventually, you will long so much for the end, because you finally will be with them all again.

"That is one of the reasons I am overjoyed to see you," Izzy said, as he shut the light and slowly walked back toward the parlor, "to pass on this responsibility. To be free of all this pressure, and now be able to move on to the next, more friendly, world."

CHAPTER 12
Summing Things Up

After an indoctrination that would have consumed three days in real time, Izzy convinced Joey he had both the duty and right to become the Keeper. Of course, two major questions persisted throughout their round-the-clock retreat: *How does the miracle making work? And why Joey Novak?*

"Why not someone who is more qualified?' Joey asked.

"Feel free to offer a few suggestions," countered Izzy, having anticipated the query since, so long ago, he had presented the same question to his wise rabbi.

"Why not some holy man, a religious person, like the Pope or Mother Teresa, or one of those TV evangelists?" Joey wondered.

"Well," Izzy replied, "the Pope is overloaded with serious global responsibilities. To do this job properly requires someone who is not in the public eye and who is able to devote considerable time to our mission. Regarding Mother Teresa. She is no longer available, since she has already passed through St. Peter's Pearly Gates. Now, as for the evangelists, would you prefer the one who was apprehended while soliciting a tainted lady of the evening, or the one who is selling God's holy healing handprint for $19.95—plus shipping and handling, and that is not available in any stores?"

Joey didn't have a reply. He sat on the stiff, Victorian-style sofa, with his hands clasped between his knees.

"Joey, Joey, I cannot tell you why Joey Novak is the new Keeper, just as I am unable to explain why Isadore Bloomwitz, an illiterate baker, was entrusted with this honor. All I can say is I learned to do it, and I have enjoyed it so very much, making people happy. And so, my young friend, will you. As for how—that part, which also to me seemed so intimidating and worrisome at the start, actually was the easiest.

"You just do it, Joey. You think, and you must pray very intensely, in order to decide when something good must be done—and if it is to be, then it occurs. In some cases, it can be immediate. Other times, the event transpires when it is most appropriate to benefit those you have chosen. There is no other way to explain it. You must do several good deeds each month. Some will be large, others will appear to be rather small. But each good act is worthwhile. You also must devote a significant amount of time in meditation and contemplation."

"You mean prayer, right?"

Smiling, Izzy nodded. "Yes, serious moments of extremely intense meditation and thoughtfulness, Joey. And we both know it is something you have stopped, primarily because you blame your God for the problems of your son."

"Let's not go there," Joey snapped.

Realizing continuing the discussion would not accomplish any good, Izzy smiled and abruptly changed the subject, leaving Joey to work through this issue on his own.

"One of the drawbacks of *my*, and now *your*, work, is that, unfortunately, you will not always be there to see the smiles and delights you have set into motion. But sometimes you will bear witness yourself. And, my young friend, when you see the thrill of happiness because of your miracle making, you will find it an indescribable and most satisfying experience. Then you will want to do it more often, which is highly encouraged."

Joey didn't reply. He just sat silently, waiting for Izzy to continue speaking, to share more of the mystery.

"Joey," the mentor said, "there are two things that you must remember. First, good intentions and money, combined with prayer, are the greatest forces of good. They can overcome all obstacles, all evil, whether it be in the form of greed, anger, malice, even physical violence. You now have all this power at your disposal, Joey. But it has consequences."

Joey had been paying close attention to Izzy's every word. Immediately, he interjected, "What does that mean?"

Izzy nodded and took a deep breath, preparing to explain. "Spending money, giving it away, is easy, Joey. You write a check, transfer funds, drop a large bill in a collection basket. Making miracles—performing unusual and much-needed good works—well, you will find the process is physically draining. The work also takes a toll on your emotional state. You will have to meditate, concentrate. It's not simple, but nothing that is worthwhile ever is. You cannot work miracles every day. It takes effort, concentration, preparation. But over time you will understand, get better at it."

"So how exactly does it work?"

"You take time to pray to your God for help, for guidance," Izzy said. "Tell Him what you want, and you'll see the results. Your monetary and miraculous resources both will work for good. But," Izzy paused and said, "remember that you are most powerful when the Kings' Coins are in your possession, readily accessible—not hidden far away at some distance and out of reach, as they have been for all these decades. They must be secure, in a safe spot, but nearby.

"Now that they are found, and in your control, your power is almost limitless. Even I, Joey, who have been without them for all these years can feel their strong influence again. Keep them safe, and keep the secret from everyone. Do you understand?"

Joey nodded. Izzy's instructions were a lot to absorb. But he still had concerns. "What if I make a mistake, do the wrong thing?"

Smiling, Izzy shook his head and replied, "That is the beauty of the Keepers' role, you cannot err, for there is a greater power guiding you, assisting you. And, if you are ever in serious doubt, call on me and I will show up and lend my opinion."

"You'll still be around?"

Letting out an exasperated sigh, Izzy explained that part of the transition of power stipulates that he must be available to assist his new charge when summoned.

"But, please, Joey, don't make a habit of it. I have a lot of catching up to do and I can't be running after you forever."

While Izzy was talking, Joey's mind had been running at high speed. He thought of the people he knew, of the needs some of them had, the good folks and the bad. Of course, there was JJ. Joey had decided that first good deed would . . . .

"No, Joey," Izzy said, his voice soft. "I know what you're planning, and it cannot be done. It would not happen despite your most persistent efforts. You cannot use the power to help yourself or those in your immediate family in a miraculous way. Your son's deafness will never be cured by you, Joey."

"Why not?" he snapped, harshly, obviously very upset.

"Because it has to be, otherwise we would become corrupted by the power at our disposal, feathering our own nests, lining our pockets. We are still human, Joey, and for all time it has been human nature to look after oneself. Power corrupts. There is no question of that.

"Consider the politicians in Washington, delegates in the U.N.," Izzy explained, "even representatives on some small town councils and bosses in companies large and small. You constantly hear horror stories about how they eventually abuse their power. Once they get comfortable in those padded chairs, they think they have the right to bend the rules for their self-interest. It starts small, and it gets worse, until bending becomes breaking—all because of greed. Eventually, the ends justify the means. They seem incapable of discerning the line between right from wrong—and if they realize the difference, they convince themselves that the rules only apply to others. They can't be reasoned with, can't be told the truth. They surround themselves with yes men and lackeys, who—for a price or promotion—agree with every stupid decision or selfish scheme the people in power come up with."

"So what's this have to do with JJ?" Joey asked, still annoyed.

Izzy sighed and said he realized Joey was frustrated he would not be able to help his son, but this one limitation to the Keeper's power was for the best. "Trust me, Joey. There are plenty of people in true need out there waiting for your help."

Although he found the situation as it related to his son to be very disappointing, it was obvious to Joey that Izzy's rules made sense.

"They are not my rules, Joey. They were established long before I was involved. I, just as you will do one day in the future, am simply passing them along. Are we clear on these matters?"

Joey nodded, then, apparently eager to get started, said, "So that's it? That's all there is to it?"

But Izzy had a few more issues to address before letting his apprentice loose. "Tomorrow morning, when you go into work, you will quit your job at the firehouse."

"WHAT?" Joey jumped out of the chair.

"Please, trust me," Izzy said. "It will be fine. You will . . . ."

"Whadaya mean fine? What am I going to live on? How will I pay my bills? This is going too far. What do you want me to say to my wife? You know she and I are not on the best of terms right now. Plus, I like my job."

"What you like is not the issue, Joey. The coins will provide. You must demonstrate your faith in me. Your financial woes are over. You will be taken care of. Just resign your full-time position tomorrow, but you must keep the bartending job, maybe even extend your hours. Uncle Lou needs your help."

Joey's tone was sarcastic and taunting, "Well, thank you, Mister Bloom. I have to quit my better job so I can work more at my part time job, where I will earn LESS money—and get no health benefits! And I am going to tell my wife that I am doing this because all of our money problems are over and I have to travel around the country doing good deeds, 'cause I got the Three Kings miracle coins. Right?"

"NO, Joey, totally wrong. You can *never*, I repeat, *never* tell your wife about the coins and your real calling. The firefighting job will interfere with your new responsibilities, but the bartending will offer you leads to those who will need your help. The work at the Inn will keep you in touch with the ordinary populace. It is actually an excellent position to gauge the pulse of people's thoughts, dreams and ideas."

"What if I say 'No'?"

Shaking his head, Izzy replied simply, "You won't. You will do everything I have directed without hesitation. Within two days, you will be shocked at the events that will transpire. Your life with your wife will be better than it has been for the past several years. Your son will love you even more. And you, my friend, Joey, will be at peace with yourself and look forward to each new day."

"So I have no choice," Joey said.

"True, not in the major direction of your role as Keeper in this human drama. But, you will be in charge regarding how you decide to help the people you select. To a degree, you will be their anonymous stage director, just as the coins and I are yours. But the recipients have free will to take your gifts and use them as they see fit. It is rather simple, really. Over time, you will find that basic good deeds are best. The less frills the better, but that realization comes with age and experience."

"And I will outlive JJ and Janice, like you and your families?"

"Probably. But we cannot be sure of what the future will hold. World events, unforeseen tragedies. These certainly may intervene with the ebb and flow and the routines of everyday life. But longevity in the Keeper position is another shortcoming of our work. And if that occurs, and you live past several generations, your life will be rich—with the sharing of good cheer and being the patriarch of many families, as opposed to just one. I envy you the many adventures you have yet to experience.

"One day, countless years from now, you will find yourself in this situation, but in the mentor role, passing the power of the coins on to another. And, please, at that time, be patient and recall how frustrated you were as you tried to comprehend the unthinkable. Also," pausing to smile, Izzy said, "I would be appreciative if you would give a kindly thought to me at that moment."

Joey smiled back at Izzy, who stood suddenly and announced it was time to go.

At the door, the older man pulled a gold ring off his finger, looked up at Joey and handed over the smooth, simple piece of jewelry. "Take this, Joey. It was hidden in the bread that my love the countess passed onto me. It will serve as an ever present reminder of your mission—to do good and to make a positive difference."

Joey took the worn yellow band and slid it onto his right hand. It was simple and smooth, with an unadorned surface. It fit perfectly. Joey thanked Izzy for the gift. They stood beside each other in silence.

"We can't change the world," Izzy said, breaking what was becoming and awkward moment, "but we can make a significant difference, at least for one person at a time. How you do that will be your decision. You will leave your mark on this Earth, Joey. You have been selected because you have a good heart. Now you have what so many people dream of, the means and power to share that goodness, to help the unlucky, the needy, the little people out there who need hope, who think they've been forgotten. But whatever you do will cause other changes, whether good or bad, that are beyond your control."

Izzy stopped talking, reached out and hugged Joey Novak. It was a warm, long, natural embrace, not awkward in any way. It was as if they were father and son, close relatives, best friends saying goodbye for the last time.

"It's time to go," Izzy said, and with his right hand he pushed Joey out through the doorway and into the dark hallway.

Joey rubbed on the ring as he started walking down the stairs. In the distance he heard a door close on the third floor. He looked at his watch. It was only 7:15 p.m. He had been in Izzy's apartment for less than an hour, but it felt like a week.

CHAPTER 13

Heading Home

It was a hot evening as Joey headed home, the car's air conditioner on high, the radio tuned to an oldies station. His mind was reeling from orientation overload, and he thought he would soon wake up from a very long bizarre and entertaining dream. Perhaps those thoughts pulled his attention away from the road. Suddenly, a small dog rushed across the street in front of his car. By the time Joey slammed on the brake, it was too late.

The screech of his tires coincided with loud, high-pitched screams. Joey looked to his right and noticed a small, blonde-headed girl, who was covering her face with two tiny hands and standing at the edge of the concrete curb.

A crowd gathered quickly as Joey opened the driver's door and ran to the front of his car, carefully pulling a small black and white puppy from beneath the right front tire. Gently, he held the dog against his chest and felt for a heartbeat, some sign of life. But the tiny animal was limp and dead.

"Is Mookie okay?" the little girl cried out from the curb. An older woman, probably her mother was wide-eyed, kneeling close beside the terrified child.

Joey looked at the woman. Their eyes met as he shook his head ever so slightly. She could tell the news was bad. There was no hope.

Turning slowly toward the mother and child, Joey began to walk with the dead dog in his arms. He went two steps before he realized this was what his new life was all about. He knew, without a doubt, at that very instant—without even listening for a heartbeat or feeling for a trace of the animal's hot breath—that Mookie could be made alive again and perfectly well.

Joey stopped walking, closed his eyes and gently pressed the lifeless dog's body tightly against his chest. Feeling the ring, Izzy's ring, on his finger, Joey prayed silently, asking God to return the gift of life to the limp animal.

As he concentrated all his thoughts, silently asking for help, Joey felt a surge of heat rush through his chest and spread down his arms, extending to his fingers. His upper body was on fire. It was nearly impossible for him to breathe. Within seconds he was able to relax and release the tension in his muscles as he sensed a surge of life leave his body and enter into the cuddly animal.

The process seemed like it consumed several few minutes, but it was over within seconds. Turning toward the small waiting group of spectators on the sidewalk, Joey, who suddenly felt light headed and very weak, tried to shout. But his voice could only reach above a whisper. "The dog's fine!" he said.

The mother's eyes displayed large question marks, but Joey could only offer a weak smile in return. Turning his face away from the woman's stare, he realized Izzy was right: *He could make good things happen. He had the power, for he was the Keeper of the Coins.* Bending slowly, he gently placed the dog on the blacktop of the street. As if it had never been injured, the animal stood erect and raced toward the arms of the crying girl.

"Now you be careful and keep him on a leash from now on," the mother directed the child as she continued to look hard at Joey, still not truly believing or fully understanding what had just happened in the street in front of her rowhouse.

It took all his remaining strength to return to his car, turn it on and drive off. Exhausted, Joey was only able to travel four blocks before he pulled off the road, parked near an abandoned factory and closed his eyes to rest and regain his strength.

It was in the moments after performing that first simple miracle that Joey realized some recipients of his goodness would question the logic of what occurred. But none, like the child's grateful mother, would ever work hard enough to negate the results of the miracles. For some inner voice would convince them they should keep the mystery of their special encounter a secret between them and the Keeper.

CHAPTER 14
Janice Is Waiting

Joey arrived home at 9 p.m. Darkness had fallen and it had been a very long day. His hopes of avoiding a highly agitated spouse and having a quiet night in his hideaway above the garage were dashed. Janice was standing on the porch, waving her arms for him to hurry into the house. Equally disconcerting was the gleaming black Cadillac with diplomatic tags consuming the length of his small driveway.

Janice was in the kitchen as Joey entered the house through the rear door. "It's about time," she snapped. "I called Uncle Lou. He said you called out tonight. Where were you?"

"Working," Joey said, wearily, as he fell into his usual chair, at the far end of the kitchen table, nearest the refrigerator. Despite Izzy's assurance that Joey's troubles were soon to be over, the late arriving husband knew it was not going to be a good evening,

"Working where?" she snapped, "at one of your many hideaway gin mills, belting down vodka shots with the guys?"

Too weary to counter her accusations, and not prepared or strong enough to dream up an explanation for his lateness, Joey gave in, offering a weak response, "Whatever, Jan. You win, all right? I was out getting sloshed, so when I came home to hear a dish full of your where-have-you-been crap I would be able to handle it. That's it. Okay, Jan? And what's with the rent-a-hearse sitting outside?"

Leaning down and making a disappointed face, his wife whispered, "No. It's not okay, Joey. And that limo out there belongs to a Mister Isadore Bloomwitz, from the Polish Consulate. He's seated in our living room. He's been waiting here for more than an hour. He's got an expensive leather briefcase across his knees, and the gentleman said he *has to see you tonight*. It's very important." Janice motioned her head in the direction of the wide doorway, leading into the small living room.

Joey was startled at hearing the name *Bloom*, and he walked slowly toward the opening to the adjacent room. Looking inside the parlor, Joey saw the visitor, who looked like the twin brother of Ichabod Crane, direct from Sleepy Hollow. The mysterious visitor was a tall, young man, well dressed in an expensive black suit. He was clutching a heavy leather valise that was resting across his lap.

"I tried to offer him coffee, a beer, soda, even hot tea. I heard somewhere that diplomats all drink tea. But he said he was 'quite fine,' in this thick accent. And that he needed to see *you*. When I said that you wouldn't be home for some time, he said he would . . . ."

"Did you say his name is Isadore Bloom?"

"No Bloomwitz, I think, why?"

"That's not Isadore Bloom," Joey said, annoyed and confused. "I never saw that guy . . . ."

"How do you know?" Jan asked. "Who's Isadore Bloom to you, anyway?"

Catching himself and vowing to be more careful, Joey waved his hand. "A guy from another firehouse that I met once. That's all. Must be a common name in Poland."

"The name is *Jewish*, Joey. Not *Polish*."

"Well, there's a lot of Polish Jews out there, too, Jan. Anyway, what the hell does the undertaker want?" Joey's voice was a strained whisper.

"Dear Lord, don't you ever listen?" Janice snapped. "Like I already told you, Joey. All he said was it was important and that he needed a *private* meeting with *you*, stressing the words *you* and *private*." Breathing out heavily, Janice added in an annoyed tone, "I guess that's his fancy way of telling me I'm *not invited*."

Assuming the visitor was a representative sent by Izzy, Joey convinced Jan to drive to the store and get a pizza for their guest. He promised to fill her in when she returned. It took only a few minutes for her to make introductions, excuse herself and head toward her car.

Joey suggested the new Mister Bloom remain seated in the relatively new overstuffed chair, located directly across from the worn sofa. A coffee table, upon which the visitor had placed his briefcase, now separated the two men. Up to that point the gentleman had not spoken and simply nodded during the introductions. When they both were settled, the diplomat asked, "Heavens, Joey, I thought you'd never get home. How long does it take to do a minor miracle on a puppy? I've been waiting with your charming wife, trying to avoid all her prying questions. What is she, a detective on the police force?"

"Welcome to my world," Joey whispered, wearily, as he looked carefully at the stranger. The face and body were different, but Joey's head jerked suddenly when he recognized the familiar, high-pitched sound of Izzy's voice.

"It's really you!" he said, pointing across the table.

A bit disappointed, Izzy frowned. "Yes, Joey. It is I, paying a follow-up visit to get things rolling and cover your tracks. So, next time don't go taking a nap downtown for an hour and then try to sort things out logically. I told you, all this is illogical in your seemingly logical world. Just have faith in me. As I stated, everything will go smoothly. But before we begin to focus on our business details, satisfy my curiosity: How did you feel tonight? When you saved the dog."

Joey shook his head. "It was wonderful. It was beautiful. But is also was just like you warned me, it was exhausting and painful. I needed to stop and rest. I felt like I hadn't slept for a week and just wanted to pass out. But the other part, how to do it, that just came to me. I had no plan. It was like being on autopilot. It felt natural. I just concentrated and prayed, very hard."

"And when you saw the results of your work? The little girl's emotion shifting from sadness to joy?"

"I just want to do it again, like you said, Izzy. It was incredible. Unbelievable. Now I . . . ."

"Believe," Izzy said, finishing his sentence. "It's about time," he muttered, opening his satchel. Shifting into business mode, he said, "Your wife will be coming in the door in about 30 seconds. She left her wallet, with her money and license, in the bedroom, but we will invite her to sit with us as I share the details that are more for her ears than yours. However, please pay close attention. You will be able to use some of the money you will be receiving to help JJ."

"I don't understand. What money? And you said I can't work any miracles to cure him."

"Right, no miracles, but you certainly can hire a tutor and have him at home with you year round from now on. Take him out of that boarding school. Or make a big donation to the deaf school up the road and he can go there. It's up to you. You can get your wife a new car, fix up the house. Move if you want to. Let Janice quit her part-time job at Sears and stay home with your son. You will need her at times to help you do some administrative work." Izzy had been talking rapidly, sounding like a manual typewriter clacking along at fast speed.

"Please, Izzy, I don't understand."

"You will, Joey. Quiet. She's back."

Joey turned his head to see Janice standing in the kitchen doorway. "Sorry," she said, shaking her head and offering an embarrassed pout. "I forgot my money. I'll be gone in a minute."

Joey and Izzy stood to acknowledge her arrival. Before her husband could speak, Izzy asked Janice to remain and witness the transaction that was about to take place. He added it was "rather positive news" that would change their lives.

As a member of the Polish Consulate in Philadelphia, Mr. Bloomwitz explained he had been directed to serve as legal representative of the Polish government. His charge was to assist in the distribution of assets of the late Janusz Jasinski, a wealthy gas and oil tycoon who had business dealings with the Polish and Russian governments.

"Jasinski was my great grandmother's name," Joey said, proudly.

"Yes, Mr. Novak, from your mother's side of the family. And, as you are the sole descendant, with no relations having been discovered in Poland or Russia, and as you have no brothers or sisters, nor cousins, and as both your parents are deceased, you are the heir to the financial assets of Janek Petro Group, Ltd., in the amount of $20 million dollars."

Janice covered her mouth with her hands and Joey fell back against the sofa. His heart started beating a bit more rapidly.

"I don't understand.You're saying we've inherited $20 million?"

"Oh, no, Mr. Novak, a significant amount more, actually. The $20 million is currently excess assets that are not needed to conduct daily business operations. There is no way to ascertain the precise amount, due to transactions by the corporate board of directors, outstanding accounts and the hourly fluctuation of oil and gas commodities."

Jan and Joey had no idea what their new best friend was saying, but since it all sounded rather positive, they remained silent, nodded and smiled.

Offering a brief polite chuckle, the diplomat tried to clear up their confusion, "In layman's terms, Mr. and Mrs. Novak, your husband has been granted the $20 million, which is committed to an interest-bearing stock and bond portfolio of that amount—designated to establish a charitable, non-profit foundation. The principal cannot be touched for at least 20 years."

The couple's excitement began to deflate, but for only a second.

"Please, allow me to finish," Mr. Bloom said. "Therefore, you will receive an annual check, based on interest income and dividends, subject to international monetary exchange values, of course."

"Of course," Joey said. "So . . . ."

"Therefore," Mr. Bloomwitz continued, "as it has taken us a few years to locate you and verify you are the sole beneficiary, I have a certified check, at this time, for $6,360,000. And . . . "

Janice could not contain herself as a small scream escaped her very dry throat.

"And," Mr. Bloomwitz said, holding up his hand, "quarterly, you, Mr. Novak—as chief operating officer of the new foundation—will receive dividends of approximately $1 to $2 million, assuming the Janek Petro Group, Ltd., maintains its current efficient operating level. Also, Mr. Novak, you will have a significant number of other responsibilities—particularly, in establishing and maintaining the foundation." Flipping through a sheaf of single-spaced, typed pages, Mr. Bloomwitz turned the thick stack of documents around and pressed his finger against the middle of one page.

"This is detailed here, on page 337 of the agreement. You also have been granted a seat on the corporate board. And, I stress this, Mr. Novak, you must attend meetings, held in the U.S. and on the continent, at various times throughout the year. Is all of this satisfactory?"

Neither Joey nor Jan replied.

"I assume from your silence that is a *Yes*," Mr. Bloomwitz said, offering a slight smile. "Now, if Mr. Novak would sign these documents of receipt and acknowledgment, I would be appreciative."

"Of course," Joey said, leaning forward, scrawling his name on more than a half-dozen pages complete with official looking, old-fashioned-style type and impressive gold seals.

"And here is your check, Mr. Novak. Now," Mr. Bloomwitz said, "I must add the following details. You must understand that the money will be sent quarterly to Mr. Novak, not jointly to you both as husband and wife. However, what you, sir, decide to do with the dividend checks—place the currency in joint accounts, separate funds—is certainly unrestricted. However, the foundation must receive a significant portion of these distributions and begin operation as soon as possible. Is that understood?"

The inner workings of Joey and Jan's minds were a drunken blur, had ceased to function. They were on confusion overload, and afraid if they asked a question this delightful and amazing dream would end. So they nodded and allowed their visitor to continue speaking at will.

"I stress it is critical that you review these stipulations carefully before making any major financial or life-changing decisions. Of course," Mr. Bloomwitz added with a tight smile, "there will be more than enough money, at present and in the future, to meet your living expenses and to allow you to achieve most of your grandest dreams."

Suddenly looking at his watch, the diplomat announced he had a pressing appointment and must leave immediately. But, he added there were a few minor details associated with the agreement that needed resolution. As he snapped the lock on his leather case and rose, he made a final directive. "If I may, Mr. Novak, I highly recommend the services of the firm of Mr. Henry Staltzmann to help you through investment issues and any tax ramifications of this windfall. He is a *close associate*, whom I have known for many, many years," Izzy said, staring directly at Joey. "Here is his card. You must visit him as soon as possible—*perhaps even early tomorrow*, Mr. Novak—to discuss a number of *critical and most pressing issues*."

Joey promised to contact the gentleman, and he and Janice walked Mr. Bloomwitz to their front door.

After the black car disappeared down the street, the stunned couple walked slowly into their home and quietly took seats on their 10-year-old, sagging sofa. In silence, their eyes glanced at worn carpets, paint-hungry walls and a 19-inch standard TV. They heard the sound of the kitchen faucet, dripping against a scuffed pot in the home's original, white porcelain sink. Janice glanced at the certified check, inked with the numerals $6,360,000, looked up at Joey and smiled.

"What are you so happy about?" he said. Abruptly, they both laughed heartily realizing the absurdity of his question.

"Well," Jan said, "tomorrow, I'm going to do three things. First, go to Sears and quit my job. Then I'm going to call JJ's school and arrange to bring him home for a long visit. Now we can afford to hire a tutor if we want and have him with us all year long. Finally, I'm going to visit Mrs. Raffel, at the Milton Loss hearing impaired school in Winslow. I want to talk to them about a large donation. If we get that school upgraded, Joey can go there and be close to home. How about you?"

Still stunned, Joey said, "I'm going to quit my job, too."

"Which one?" Jan said.

"Just the firehouse one, I think," he said. "I still want to help Uncle Lou at the Inn. He's getting up there, and I'm sure he could use the help."

"Good," Janice said. "I don't need you underfoot and bumping into me all day long while I'm redecorating—or maybe looking for a new house, and a new car, and who knows what else."

CHAPTER 15

Going to Work

Upon arriving at the firehouse, Joey had planned to ask for a brief meeting with his lieutenant. However, a note taped to his locker informed him that the officer in charge needed a brief meeting with Joey.

It took less than five minutes for Joey to learn that city cutbacks had forced the department to suspend 60 firefighters. He was among the unfortunates to be sent home that day, with two months severance pay and a promise to be placed toward the top of the list when funds were found to rehire the much needed staff.

After a breakfast at a local diner, he walked to Walnut Street and stopped in front of a metal sign identifying the high-rise complex as the "Staltzmann Building." After flashing the business card that Mr. Bloomwitz had given him the night before, a uniformed doorman directed Joey to the express elevator reserved to transport special clients directly to the 34th floor. When Joey exited the elevator, he found himself in the lobby of Henry Staltzmann's legal, financial and corporate consulting firm.

The staff at the center city penthouse office treated Joey like visiting royalty. In fact, it seemed both the receptionist and Mr. Staltzmann had been expecting his arrival.

Mr. Staltzmann, who insisted on being called "Henry," had a dark complexion and a mane of thick, slick, combed back, 1950s-style hair. His office, which was decorated with a dozen fresh flower arrangements, smelled like a funeral parlor. The attorney/accountant looked like a six-foot-tall beanpole. Joey figured the man couldn't weigh more than 120 pounds—in a soaking wet snowsuit. Apparently, Henry already had a copy of Joey's documents. The legal expert, who had been highly recommended by Izzy-in-disguise went over the lengthy agreement and boiled it down into plain English.

"According to this," Henry said, "you don't have to do a single thing except sit back and await your bank deposits and wire transfers.

It seems your late night visitor has explained the board meetings and your responsibilities in front of your wife, so she is to assume you will be operating in a traditional work setting. However, in fact, you will be in this or other communities of your choosing, performing your new and rather untraditional mission. Is this clear?"

Joey nodded his head, then replied in a soft, hesitant voice, "Look, I'm new at this. I don't understand very much, except that I was sent to you, apparently to help me with the legal end of things."

"Mr. Novak," Henry said, slightly rolling his eyes, "I am fully associated with the overall project. However, to my staff members you are simply another wealthy philanthropist client. For the last several months, I have been aware that a new Keeper was expected, so it is not necessary to be hesitant or concerned with my awareness of what others might consider your *rather peculiar* situation.

"In fact, I had known Mr. Bloom for quite some time. I will admit that at one point, about six years ago, he had become frustrated, since you had not discovered the coins and his message. Within the last two days, I have been alerted that you would be making a visit to our firm soon. So we prepared for your arrival."

Taking off his glasses and resting them atop his desk, Henry said, "If I may, allow me to summarize the situation, and it is quite simple. Your responsibility is to spend the money you have inherited helping others that you select as worthy of your generosity. Basically, you must perform good deeds with these assets. If your wife ever phones your office number—which is connected to my assistant Samantha's phone, in our reception lounge—she will answer 'Mr. Novak's Foundation,' or whatever you want to name your nonprofit organization. We are here, Mr. Novak, to be of assistance and, quite often, serve as a cover story for your whereabouts or activities.

"We even have a suite of offices for you in a wing on this floor, and we're waiting to paint the foundation's name in gold letters on the doors. This is your legal headquarters of record. But, as I understand things, you are not supposed to spend much time here."

"I know," Joey said. "I'm really going to be out, wherever—in New York, South America, L.A., Vegas, Timbuktu—spreading goodness and cheer year round. I guess I sort of think of my new job as a modern day, year round Kris Kringle, without the sleigh. And if the new Mrs. Kringle asks, you're to say I'm away at a board meeting, locally or overseas, depending on my needs. Right?"

"Correct, Mr. Novak."

"Please," the younger man asked, "can you please call me Joey? I'd like that a lot. All right? Deal?"

Nodding ever so slightly, Henry replied, reluctantly, "I will try."

"Fine. So can I have you write the checks, send out the money, do all the paperwork? I'm not good at keeping records and receipts. I got into a little trouble with the IRS, some years back, over cash income from a dog cart operation. I was in it with two other guys from the firehouse. We had a mobile operation. Thought we had a primo location—on a corner near city hall. And we did kids' parties and craft fairs and stuff on the weekends. But it was a bust. Hell, I still got the cart. It's sittin' there rusting away behind Uncle Lou's garage. Whole damn thing turned out to be a freakin' nightmare. Ya know what I mean?"

Henry smiled and replied. "Yes We will take care of all the paperwork. That's what we do. In fact, Joey, we are at your disposal 24 hours each day, seven days a week. One of our staff is always on call, and frequently I will respond promptly and personally to your needs."

"Sounds fine to me," Joey said, "But then I guess you know how all this stuff is handled. I mean, that's your job. But give me a few more answers, and then I'm on my way. First, I'd like to know: How much can I spend?"

"As much as you want."

"All $6 million?"

"Actually," Henry explained, "much more. You have an unlimited line of credit, which our firm can cover. Since you are being guided, indirectly, of course, you cannot make a serious error. You simply tell us what you want accomplished—in a financial sense—and we will send out the checks or call the appropriate parties to make things happen."

Joey nodded, then asked for the morning paper.

Henry pressed a button and requested that one of his assistants bring the *Philadelphia Inquirer* into his office.

Pointing to the story at the bottom of page one, below the fold, Joey said, "They just cut 60 firefighters, including me. I figure that they need about $2.4 million, which should probably cover pay and benefits, to keep them on the job for a year. Can you do it?"

Squinting slightly at the newspaper story, Henry said, "I see you are beginning to understand your responsibilities. Yes, we will take care of it. However, I suggest we offer an anonymous donation to the city, but we also make it public—put it on the evening news, TV and radio. Of course, we will not use any names. By going public, we will pressure the city into matching our generous amount with $5 million of its own. That will insure a three-year commitment for the affected personnel, giving them a better sense of job security. I know the city has more than that amount in one of its unrestricted reserve securities. For them, it is like earning 50 percent interest on their money, which currently is probably at 8 to 11 percent at best. They won't be able to turn it down.

"I will make some calls, behind the scene, alert the proper people in finance, then one of our people will leak certain details to highly placed municipal union representatives and members of the media. That will get them involved in the process. The deal will be confirmed in time to make the late night news and be on tomorrow morning's front page. Do I have your permission, Mr., I mean, Joey?"

"Do it," Joey said, smiling at the ease of getting things done.

"It's as good as done," Henry said, shaking Joey's hand as they rose from their chairs near the desk.

"We do need a name for your foundation," Henry said.

"I was thinking about that last night, when Izzy mentioned it at the house. How about Melchior?"

"Melchior," Henry said, making a note of it on a pad. "I will have my staff research corporate records to see if it is available. Any significance I should be aware of?"

"No. Just a neat name I sorta like," Joey said. "Well," he added, almost embarrassed, "to be honest, it's the name of one of the three kings. The one who brought the gold."

Henry smiled. "Very appropriate. We'll get on it right away. If it is obtainable, we will order your business cards and have a painter begin work on your door. Any preference in furniture? Contemporary or classical styles? Light or dark wood? Perhaps you prefer composites? What about carpeting, any particular hue?"

Joey paused. He was confused and not really interested in how his office looked. If he was in charge he'd probably put in a pool table, wet bar and paint all the walls Eagles green and white.

"How about if you call my wife down? Let her decide. She likes to decorate. I'll be fine with whatever she picks. Maybe you could have her work with somebody from your office. All right?"

Smiling, Henry agreed to have one of his staff arrange for Janice to visit soon.

"One thing," Joey added, "don't let her put up any of that abstract crap that looks like some preschool kids tossed a can of paint against a wall from a moving car. I'm more of a tall ships, lighthouse in a storm kind of guy."

"No problem," Henry said. "I understand completely."

As the accountant grasped the knob to show Joey out, the visitor paused and said, rather softly, "I've also got this little problem, having to do with a lawyer."

Henry let out a soft chuckle and waved a hand in the air, "Done. We contacted Mr. Julian MacElvery III—a rather minor, ambulance-chasing attorney—this morning. Speaking on your behalf, we threatened to go public with his repulsive antics at the baseball game. And we also promised to make public the abuse case he lost against his ex-wife five years ago in San Antonio. We have pictures of her injuries secured from her attorney. Not surprisingly, Mr. MacElvery became very cooperative. He is dropping his demands and will be sending you and your son a letter of apology. In addition, he will buy new uniforms for the team and make a $5,000 donation to the midget league, or to another worthy charity of your choice. Do you have any other concerns related to this matter?"

Relieved, but noticing he was no longer surprised by the way things were being resolved, Joey said, "Last question, for today: How long have you known Izzy?"

Henry offered a weak smile and replied, "What a wonderful gentleman. All my life, until he died four years ago."

Shocked, Joey replied, "That's impossible. I just spent the last three days with him. He was at my house last night!"

"No, Joey," Henry replied, "I'm sorry, but that's highly unlikely." But, after a few seconds of thought, the accountant raised his eyebrows and added, "Then, again, with Izzy, anything is possible."

Chapter 16

Return Visit

Much had been accomplished in a short amount of time that morning, and it was still well before noon when Joey rang the bell at Izzy's Sansom Street apartment. After his visit with Henry, Joey had become more confused and found he had additional questions for his mentor that needed to be answered.

After waiting at the door several minutes and getting no response, he entered the adjacent Jewelers' Row showroom of Jerry Lublin's Diamond Mine. The store occupied the first level of Izzy's building.

There were only two customers, but many more would arrive during the lunch hour, in the early evening and on the weekend. Daytime, primarily, was catch-up time for many of the jewelry store owners, who had their staffs calling in orders, checking with other dealers to fill special requests and restocking display cases.

Only two salespeople were working the floor, and since they both were occupied, Joey took a few moments to wander around the shop. Rather than focusing on the gems displayed under shatterproof glass, he studied the framed award certificates and faded newspaper articles decorating the walls.

Gemologists Association of America honors were interspersed with stories honoring Lublin's employees and owners. One thin black frame caught Joey's eye. Stretching his body forward, across the counter, he tried to read the obituary below the headline: "Jerry Lublin, store founder, well known diamond merchant dies."

In the small box surrounded by laudatory copy was the tiny face of Izzy Bloom, the former resident of the apartment two floors above. Joey squinted his eyes, trying to decipher the tiny type that recorded the highlights of the man's life story.

Noting the visitor's efforts, a middle age man approached, took down the framed story and handed it to Joey, "It's easier for you to read now," he said, smiling. "Just drop it off when you're done. I'll be in that side office, next to the front door."

"Thanks," Joey replied, as he looked down and slowly read the obituary of his mentor's life. The article was dated four years earlier.

It praised Jerry Lublin, long-time diamond merchant, for his attention to detail and loving disposition. The story listed more than a dozen organizations to which he claimed membership. He was found dead in his third floor, Sansom Street apartment owned by the Lublin Corporation. Funeral services were private, and no cemetery was mentioned. There were no details on his age or relations.

The article was a good size, more than a quarter of the page. In a city of several million people, not everyone who died received as much ink as Izzy. And, apparently proud of its deceased founder, Izzy/Lublin's obit had earned a place of honor on a wall in the store.

No clues here, Joey thought as he turned and knocked on the partially closed door to return the framed death announcement to the manager.

"Come in," said a familiar voice. It was an invitation Joey could not decline.

Taking a seat in the cramped, closet-like room, Joey looked at the large, unfamiliar face, but with a very recognizable voice, and hesitantly whispered, "It's you again."

Smiling, the man nodded, and Izzy's voice replied, "I figured you'd show up here, snooping around, wanting to get another look at the apartment. Well, the answer's NO! I've had to adjust my schedule because I knew you would be wanting more information, especially after meeting with Henry."

"But he said you've been dead for . . . . "

"Four years, correct! I couldn't hold out and wait forever for you to arrive. When you found the coins they sent me back—on temporary assignment—to train you. But we have to stop meeting like this. I have to be heading on, and your puttering and foot dragging is beginning to annoy me."

"But I don't understand how you could be dead, and now here?"

Frustrated, Izzy let out a huge sigh. "Listen very carefully, Joey. I repeat. *You are trying to apply logical reasoning to an illogical situation*! The other evening you accepted suspended time, you brought a dog back to life, you received more than six million dollars—and now you are having a problem comprehending my return from the Great Beyond? Please, suspend your long-held beliefs and accept that you are the main character in a very peculiar situation—and learn to live with it! All right?"

Joey didn't reply. He just stared at the manager's face. It was difficult hearing Izzy's voice coming from the stranger's lips.

"And get used to my appearance, too," Izzy said, reading Joey's confused mind. "I might come back as a bird one day and sit on your shoulder and start whispering in your ear. Now, if that happened, you would have something to fret about. Finally, is there anything else you need me to handle before you accept *your new life* so I am allowed to move on with *my life*?"

Joey shook his head.

A bit irritated, Izzy snapped, "Well, after all the time I've spent with you, sharing all I learned over the centuries, a word of thanks certainly would be in order."

"Thanks," Joey said, weakly.

"A bit more enthusiasm would be appreciated. It took a lot of planning to execute that diplomatic stunt to make things believable with your wife. Then I had Henry terrify that idiot lawyer you assaulted in the park. And you, in your haste, just spent about $3 million to bail out the city fire department."

"You said I should jump right in."

"Yes, I did, but don't throw the money around like a drunken sailor. Leave a little for rest of the world that you have to save."

Joey nodded. "How come you keep showing up? I thought you wanted to move on?"

"I do. But you have questions. Too many, in fact. And I have to respond to them. They just can't send someone else, because there is no one else. It's just you and me. Until it's you and someone else, later. Much later."

"How will I know when, and how did you know it was necessary to hide the coins?"

"Ah, I knew that one would come up. We didn't cover that in our first meeting or the brief second encounter in your living room. I had sent the coins forward to prevent them from falling into the hands of the Nazis, just as you would do the same if, in the future, you had serious concerns about their safekeeping. But, trust me, you will know if the situation warrants such a bold move, and you will decide and make plans to do so, in your own fashion. And, please get those coins out of that Chock Full o' Nuts tin can and place them somewhere more secure. I've had visions about some child digging them up and using them to buy ice cream from a Mister Softee truck."

Joey promised to rent a safety deposit box and move them.

"Who's Jerry Lublin? Is that your name?"

"I've gone by many different names, depending upon the situation. I've assumed a number of identities, even," Izzy paused and smiled, "a diplomat, when necessary. Jerry Lublin is a name I thought up when I opened this enterprise. It had a nice ring to it, back in the 1950s, anyway. Dean Martin and that nut Jerry Lewis were hot then. I figured Jerry sounded friendly, that it would make people feel comfortable. I didn't want people coming into a place called Bloom's Rings and Things. Sounds like a florist or a garden center. So I used Lublin, the name of my hometown and that's how it happened.

"That," Izzy said with a tone of finality, "I think answers all of your outstanding queries. And I hope there are no more, for I am becoming impatient and desire to head off."

Joey sat for a moment, said nothing, his face staring at the floor. Slowly, he raised his head, faced Izzy and said, "I think that's it. I'm ready. I really feel it. You can go, Izzy. Thank you."

"Hallelujah, Lord! Finally, I am headed back to the promised land," he replied jokingly. "Now, don't look so glum. Henry can address and respond to most of your needs, and I am only a prayer away." Izzy stood. He was tall, in the form of the store manger, a heavy man with a bubble-like head and thin layer of gray hair. But the eyes were the same, full of fire and zeal, and Izzy's ornery sort of kindness. He put out his hand, gripped Joey's tightly and said, "Good luck, Keeper. Be safe and work some wonderful miracles." Then Izzy paused, looked seriously at Joey and added, "But remember this, money can only do so much, and it won't always solve the problem."

"What do you mean?" Joey asked.

"Look at the lottery winners. They become millionaires, and just a few years later they're miserable, they're broke, their families won't talk to them because they've become jealous of the winners' wealth and fame. At times, money is more of a problem than a solution. So you have to be sure to . . . "

"To use the other stuff, the good power you talked about—to meditate, to make sure the real problems are solved. Right?'

Izzy smiled, pleased that his apprentice seemed to understand there was going to be more to the Keepers' job than unlimited riches could buy. "Right, Joey. And just as I and others before me learned by doing, so will you. But, remember, miracle working is overwhelming. It's exhausting. So take it slowly."

Joey was surprised at the affection he had developed for someone he had known only a few days. It was as if they were close relations, saying goodbye for the last time. Instinctively, Joey moved forward, wrapped his arms around the larger man's body and hugged him tightly.

Suddenly, Joey was startled as the frightened store manger tried to pull away, shouting, "Sir! Sir! Please, let go! Please!" The voice was deep, different. No longer the mentor's familiar squeak.

Embarrassed, Joey stepped back, realizing Izzy was gone, and in leaving abruptly the mentor had played another of his jokes on Joey.

"It was nothing, sir," the jeweler said, quickly stepping away from Joey. "It's nothing to become emotional over. I just let you read the obituary."

Red faced and annoyed, Joey mumbled an incomprehensible and weak apology as he raced out of the showroom, vowing never to enter Lublin's Diamond Mine in any of his several upcoming lifetimes.

CHAPTER 17

Regulars at the Inn

Uncle Lou was delighted when Joey said he had lost his job at the firehouse and that the younger man wanted to work more hours at the family business. In fact, worried that his nephew might change his mind, Lou hurriedly hung up his apron, offered a brief wave and left the building at 2 p.m. He was a bald, heavy-set, barrel-chested man, but when necessary he moved with unexpected swiftness for his large size. This was one of those moments. Joey's uncle was thrilled to be able to head off to Atlantic City four hours earlier than usual. Without hesitation or the slightest concern, he left his newly appointed, full-time manager in charge of the bar and disappeared.

As the midday hours moved toward darkness, Joey witnessed the daily procession of the Welcome Inn's regulars and strangers—each one sharing tales of dreams dashed and their elusive goals still awaiting achievement.

Tuning out several simultaneous streams of various customers' conversations—that ranged from silly to serious to downright stupid—Joey surveyed the interior boundaries of his new kingdom.

The corner rowhouse dwelling had been built about a hundred years before and was designed to host a business. Through the first six decades of the 20th century, there were hundreds of similar family-owned enterprises commanding coveted corner-of-the-block locations in every neighborhood in the city. Each store also had an apartment unit on the second-level, which was occupied by the owner and his family. Uncle Lou still lived in the same rooms where Joey's grandparents had eaten, slept and raised their brood of first-generation American children.

The small corner stores housed a variety of businesses—groceries, shoemaker and tailor shops, cleaners, soda fountains, bakeries and newsstands. You could live in one of these neighborhood villages your entire life and never need a car. The trolley would provide access to downtown's larger department stores and on a daily basis you could walk to purchase anything needed. But by far the friendly neighborhood saloon—also called a tavern, gin mill, beer garden and cafe—was the most popular destination. Decades ago, there were more bars per block than grocery stores and bakeries. Sometimes, all four corners of an intersection hosted a quartet of competing and always-busy gin mills or private drinking clubs.

The Welcome Inn's interior was typical of your basic, dimly lit local watering hole. To the left of the entrance was a small, 10-stool bar, behind which the owner/barkeep watched over his domain. Within easy reach behind the bar was an oversized wooden club—called the "Enforcer," "Judge" or "Persuader." This was the owner's silent partner, which he displayed when things began to get a bit out of hand. Often, just raising the "Judge" would defuse a tense situation.

Along either side of the center aisle running the length of the building were small two-seater tables, or worn leather booths hugging the walls that could hold up to four. Regulars had their favorite spots—mostly along the bar. The second tier of familiar customers, who also were known on a first-name basis, commanded tables near the front door. And woe to anyone who dared, even by accident, to sit on someone's preferred stool or chair.

The Inn's main wall displayed four framed color pictures, which had been cut carefully from the *Daily News* or the Sunday *Inquirer's* weekly magazine. Each photo was bordered in a five-and-dime metal frame. They hung in an uneven row above the coffin-shaped, metal beer box. In Uncle Lou's mind, only John F. Kennedy, Pope John Paul II, Ronald Reagan and John Wayne had reached a level of respect that deserved a space on his personal wall of fame.

During the eight decades the Welcome Inn had operated since its speakeasy days during Prohibition, multiple layers of wafting smoke from cheap cigars and filterless cigarettes had been absorbed in its pine-paneled walls. Every corner bar patron recognized the distinctive smell that was a combination of old smoke, stale beer and spilled alcohol.

The slightly pungent essence immediately attacked the senses as a customer crossed the front door threshold. But it wasn't an unpleasant experience. The aroma was a silent signal to members of the bar family that they had arrived home—entered a haven where they would be safe, comfortable and accepted. No matter what they thought, no matter how wacky they acted or how bizarre their crazy comments might seem to the outside world, in the Inn they could relax and just be themselves.

For years it was a unwritten, but universal, bar rule that religion and politics were forbidden topics of conversation—because of the arguments they would generate. However, any regular knew if you mixed enough alcohol with any topic, in a flash the combination could ignite a verbal or physical confrontation.

As if to prove the point, at a table near the edge of the bar Buddy Bassdard—owner of a brake repair shop near the airport, who had an uncanny resemblance to Mr. Clean—was heatedly arguing a point with JFK (Jackson Fletcher King)—a city sanitation worker, who could pass for Mike Tyson's twin. The black man had a habit of mentioning that he had the same initials as the assassinated president, whose smiling image hung just above Jackson's head. It didn't take a Rhodes Scholar to realize that if the two muscled men, who were sharing a table and an animated discussion, decided to go at it, Uncle Lou would have to rebuild, not just remodel, the front section of the Inn.

"I ask ya, Bassdard," JFK stated firmly, "What's the most ya ever put down in one night?"

Glaring across the table, Buddy eyed his drinking partner, trying to determine if there was some hidden agenda behind the question. Being cautious, he looked at JFK and tossed out several questions of his own. "Are we talkin' length of time here, or are we talkin' straight alcohol or beer? If it's the hard stuff, are we lookin' at on the rocks or straight up? Do you mean in one sittin' without takin' a leak? Or do you get an unlimited number of pit stops? Is there food involved or not? I mean, hell, that's a loaded question, JFK. No way I can answer without you givin' up some guidelines."

Shaking his head, JFK said, "I ain't tryin' to paint yer ass into no corner, Bassdard. I was just makin' conversation."

"Bullshit!" Buddy snapped, without warning. His deep voice sounded like an exploding cannon. "I know when the hell you're up to somethin' And I ain't no fool."

Frowning, JFK muttered something uncomplimentary about his tablemate, suggesting that Buddy's family name was right on the mark, and that the brake mechanic continued to live up to the Bassdards' notorious heritage.

"Screw you!" Buddy snapped back, his face the color of Texas Pete hot sauce, "I know what you're getting' at. Don't think I don't. It's that damn mug isn't it?" Buddy shouted, as he pointed at the gigantic red and brown beer stein on a shelf above the center of the back bar.

Beginning to laugh, JFK smiled at his drinking companion and slyly said, "It might be." Then he flashed a wide smile, showing off his pearly whites that were accented with a half dozen gold caps.

Buddy took a swallow of his long neck, slammed down the bottle and glared.

The object of his sensitivity was a legendary incident that had occurred in the Inn on a Friday evening, two years earlier. Late that afternoon, immediately after work, Buddy Bassdard had challenged anyone willing to put up a bet of any size that he could drink a full case of beer—24 cans—before midnight. Earlier in the week, he had confirmed that the huge decorative stein could hold exactly two dozen cans of liquid refreshment. Therefore, when Buddy achieved the feat, he could claim he had consumed all the beer the monster mug could hold.

Bets were taken, a larger than usual crowd gathered and Buddy started off with a bang. In the first hour, ending at 6 p.m., he had downed eight cans and only had 16 to polish off in the remaining six hours. But as time ticked by, his guzzling pace slowed down to a trickle. By 10 p.m., the Bassdard had made several mad dashes into the men's room—as laughter, jeers and cheers around the bar accompanied the sound of Buddy's heaving and moaning.

But to the surprise of many doubters, the bald beer-athoner was down to only three 12-ounce brews at 11:10 p.m. In a moment of bravado, Buddy announced he only needed to swill 36 ounces in 50 minutes. "Hell!" Buddy slurred, "that's less than an ounce a minute. Any candyass can drink that much." But then he made a calculated error. Looking at the three beer cans and the healthy pile of cash in the betting pool, his grog-clouded brain convinced Buddy that he could win it all. Full of confidence, the Bassdard offered to double the bets of anyone who was brave enough to lay down more green.

Of course, Buddy couldn't hear his slurred speech, couldn't see the way he weaved and bobbed around the room, couldn't notice the glazed film that spread across his rolling eyes, couldn't feel the thin stream of hops descending from his bottom lip.

Everyone but Buddy knew that within minutes the bold Bassdard's body would be kissing the Welcome Inn's floor.

Making sure they didn't miss out on a "sure thing," compliments of a greedy Bassdard, money flew, cheers roared and smiles beamed. The merry spectators were eager to cash in on this once-in-a-blue-moon, gambling gift.

Suddenly, Buddy grabbed one of the remaining cans of brew. It was 11:20 p.m. "Down she goes!" he shouted, as the contents in the silver aluminum container of Budweiser, the Bassdard's brew of choice, disappeared inside the contestant's mouth. The room was silent as a church during the Consecration. Looks of awe and respect covered the faces of those who had bet big against Buddy. If he could perform the consumptive feat two more times, he would become a beer garden myth, on a par with the legendary gods of Greece and Rome. And he would stuff his pockets with more bills than he would earn in a month at his day job. A career on the road as a competitive beer drinker was not unthinkable.

But on this Friday night, the Bassdard's story would not conclude with a happy ending. His quest would remain an impossible dream.

In a corner bar, with two-dozen silent witnesses, Buddy's large, bald-headed body suddenly became statuesque. The empty can fell from his hand and clanged against the floor, only one second before his massive frame crashed against the bar's wooden surface.

Some witnesses described it as the sound of a large tree falling in a forest. A lone voice—it's believed belonging to JFK—shouted out "TIMBER!" signaling the end of both the evening's entertainment and Buddy's dream.

The betters grabbed their winnings. Uncle Lou cleaned up the bar, and a few regulars dragged the Bassdard's limp body into the men's room—where he slept and wretched throughout the night.

For months afterwards, tales of Buddy's failed quest circulated throughout neighborhood clubs and saloons. And distant shouts of "TIMBER!" would be heard whenever he entered a room. Although no one was dumb enough to mock the Bassdard to his face.

At their table in the Inn, Buddy glared at JFK and snarled, "You think you're funny, bringin' that shit up. Don't ya?"

But JFK couldn't answer. He was too busy trying not to choke on his drink. It was obvious he enjoyed raising Buddy's blood pressure. Trying to diffuse the mounting tension, JFK said, "Hey, lighten up, man. You're the only guy I know that's named after a damn fallin' tree. I mean, hell. That was some night to reme'ber. But then," JFK added with a smirk, "ya pra'bly don't reme'ber much of that night at all. Right?"

Buddy had reached his limit. Standing up, he shouted, "Ya know, they shot the real JFK in '63. Maybe somebody will do us another favor and take you out. Whatdaya think of that? Ya damn, wise mouthed . . ."

From his stool behind the bar, Joey sensed things at the table were getting way out of hand. Grabbing two cold, 7-oz. bottles of Rolling Rock, he moved swiftly toward the scene of the beer guzzling controversy. Dropping a pair of green-bottled frosties between the two arguing men, Joey suggested they take it easy and enjoy the beers, on the house, of course.

With that minor brushfire dowsed and the over-sized opponents seated and enjoying their complimentary brews, Joey returned to his post and did a quick survey of the rest of the room.

Donna, who was heading out the door, turned and offered a quick wave and smile. She worked as a waitress at the South Street Diner. A single mother in her late thirties, for years she'd been hoping for child support she would never receive and searching the want ads for a higher paying job—one with better hours, some benefits and someplace located closer to home.

Jersey Jack was perched on his barstool nearest the door. The 62-year-old, crew-cut-wearing truck driver from the Garden State was an ex-Marine and known for offering bargains for cheap—consisting mainly of merchandise he had *salvaged* after it had been damaged or lost—from *falling off the loading dock*. Last month it was a case of double D-cup, orange brassieres and a crate of lime-colored stuffed alien dolls. This week's special was a half-dozen cartons of bright blue-and-silver umbrellas, sporting the Dallas Cowboy logo—certainly not a popular, must-have item in Philly.

Long John was sitting on the stool beside Jack. The 72-year-old, retired union plumber, who was shaped like the Michelin Tire Man, spoke with a lisp whenever he got excited. To look at him, few would realize he had an interest in Chinese art and symphonic music—and each year he bought a season ticket to the Philadelphia Orchestra's weekly matinee concert series.

Cliff the Coach was alone in the back of the room, slumped in a booth near the small sink and restrooms. He had worked for decades as a high school assistant football coach. The sad-eyed man taught driver's ed and dreamed of landing a head coaching position. But, at age 59, he knew he was past the age when any school would express interest in his experience and abilities. So he spent each fall Friday night as a sideline bridesmaid, and with each passing quarter his chances of catching the pigskin bouquet became less likely.

Maurice, one of the younger customers had passed Donna at the door as he entered. A medical student and part-time taxi driver, he used the Inn as his rest stop and private library. Often commandeering a quiet corner booth and nursing a light beer, he studied textbook formulas and clinical charts, but was frequently interrupted by customers seeking free medical advice.

Father Tom, an ex-priest who had been associated with one of the lesser-known Catholic sects, was a three-times-a-week regular. Joey expected the friendliest of his regulars to arrive at any time. If his usual booth was taken, he calmly moved to another, making no fuss. Many customers speculated he was a closet alcoholic, who had been defrocked for an addiction to booze. Nevertheless, the cleric was the bar's most popular human fixture, offering free counseling and a receptive ear. The Inn was his outreach mission, and the regulars were his flock.

While those made up the core of the Inn's main cast, other supporting characters passed through the revolving entry door on a less frequent basis. Some were known by their hobbies or occupations. Nicknames were the rule and surnames were rarely known.

There was Motorcycle Mike (owner of a bike shop), Gutterman (new drainpipes and aluminum gutters, a specialty), Jimmy the Mailman (who never missed a delivery), Accordion Man (an elderly musician, who often brought along his raggedy-looking squeezebox and eagerly performed a tune for whomever would listen), Mister Freeze (an unpopular bookmaker, who rarely made a payoff), John the Engineer (as in trains, not high technology) and Ray the Spray (the neighborhood exterminator, who gave off a pungent chemical smell, ensuring barstools adjacent to his would remain vacant and allow him ample elbow-bending room).

Certainly, passing travelers with no deep roots to the Inn were at least tolerated, but Joey knew he would begin to anticipate and enjoy the arrival of his regulars. Their zany experiences made slow days pass a bit more rapidly. Plus this varied cast shared its plights and delights with every shot and beer.

But he wondered if his arrival as the Inn's new manager was something more. Perhaps, Joey thought, his presence at the rundown, corner beer garden was a crucial part of Izzy's master plan. What better setting to maintain a solid connection with the working class, the people who lived from day to day, the poor slobs who hoped and dreamed, but who knew that Lady Luck, or the generous leprechaun with the pot of gold. would never find them? That their ship would never come in.

Over time, Joey realized, this saloon and its extended family—of clowns and misfits, these well-meaning, down-on-their-luck, good-hearted friends—would provide information and leads about people in genuine need. And they would be some of the people who would benefit from the Keeper's newfound good fortune.

Chapter 18

Seeking Out the Needy

It was the end of October, a little more than a month since Joey's first meeting with Izzy. The firefighter turned philanthropist had not yet fallen into a rhythm. He was still uncomfortable in his new vocation, and he realized he was going to have to spend considerable time trying to identify beneficiaries of his talents.

Janice as well had taken to their new life. Certainly, they were able to afford material items that had been unthinkable only weeks before. They had agreed to stay in their home, but Janice did redecorate their house and also spent time working on Joey's new offices. She made major donations to the Milton Loss Academy, the local school for the hearing impaired, and was named chairperson of its newly formed Rebuilding Committee. Making the school a better place for JJ and the other students became her primary interest, and it was one that took considerable time.

With his wife relatively happy, with JJ living at home—and going to the local school and working with a tutor—Joey was able to spend time each day with his son. And that, more than anything, he realized, had been Izzy's major gift to him.

* * *

Since it was a slow weekday at the Inn, Joey finished his early morning setup. Sitting in a chair behind the bar, he pulled a maroon leather bound journal from his briefcase. Soon after his life had changed, he had decided to keep a record of his work. After a month's time, Joey was amazed at what he had not been able to accomplish.

In the muted light of the back bar, at a few minutes before the daily 9 o'clock opening, he ran his finger down the carefully hand written pages. It was a rather poor legacy, but, Joey told himself, it was only a beginning.

Of course, Mookie the dog was his most special experience, mainly because it was his first achievement. That was followed by the settlement of the sudden city fire department workforce reduction. The first was a minor miracle that sapped his physical strength. The second, a hefty $2.5 million giveaway that was as easy as making a quick decision. Henry had taken care of the other details and Joey moved on to others in need.

A week later, he had arranged for a home to be given to the elderly couple who were burned out of their trailer while visiting their daughter. They were older folks, had no insurance and their story was the lead feature on the 11 o'clock news. It wasn't hard to locate them, and Henry again processed the paperwork.

Another situation demanded nothing more of Joey than writing a check. Through a private detective Henry had hired, a dying mother in Boston was reunited on her hospital deathbed with the daughter the woman had given up for adoption at birth.

After reading a story in the Sunday paper, Joey bought an aging textile factory in North Carolina. The mill was the sole employer of a town, and Joey's purchase stopped the jobs from being transferred overseas. With the hefty annual subsidy Henry had suggested, the declining business operation would allow at least one more generation to work, and keep the small mountain village from dying a slow painful death.

During those weeks, Joey had tossed lots of money into beggars' cups and church collection plates. Almost feeling guilty that his millions were sitting idle, he directed Henry to send hefty donations from the Melchior Charitable Trust to several reputable charitable agencies.

Throughout the day and night Joey scanned the Internet and newspapers for worthy candidates. He hardly slept and instead watched the 24-hour news channels for segments spotlighting folks in need. But he was unsatisfied, not comfortable with his situation. He continually compared himself to a child trying to walk. He didn't believe he was on solid ground. After a few steps forward, with each minor success, he seemed to fall down and question whether his actions had been the right choice. He wondered if he had handled things in the correct manner.

But there was no one to talk to; no one to provide feedback. The Keepers' secret had to remain hidden from everyone.

Joey knew he would eventually figure things out for himself. He would learn by doing. He also realized his charge was to do much more than throw money at the problems he identified. It was just that he was still afraid to use his miracle-making talents, and was particularly concerned that he would select the wrong situation or make some stranger's very serious problems even worse.

Chapter 19

'Do You Believe in Miracles?'

November was supposed to be cold, but not deliver the bitter blasts of bone-chilling frost that usually arrived in January. Every time the Inn entrance door opened, a whoosh of frigid wind seemed to push the next customer into the waiting warmth of the dark, welcoming watering hole.

The stranger at the bar was an average-sized man, not too tall and not too short. Not overweight and not skinny. Just typical. He dressed like a professional, but was certainly not a wealthy businessman—more like a harried salesman or an underpaid schoolteacher. Just a guy who who needed a place to hide out and regroup for a few minutes. He looked neat. Polite. Not the type of customer who would cause you to take a second glance, or make you think he might create a problem.

He arrived just as the lunch crowd was finishing up their sandwiches and drinks, heading back to their respective worksites, hoping the clock would move swiftly toward quitting time. But this first-time patron was in no mood to move on. He seemed content to settle in for a spell.

A veteran bartender knows when a fellow wants to talk, share a sad story or seek free advice across the counter.

Tapping his empty glass twice with the edge of his ring, the stranger summoned Joey over and asked for another cold one. A draft.

As Joey delivered the beer, the fellow passed a fiver across the top of the bar and said, "Keep the change."

Joey thanked him and began to turn.

"Got a minute, pal?" the nice dresser asked.

"Got all day. I'm already at work," Joey said. He hated when people called him *pal*.

The dresser looked around the room. Long John was the only other person sitting at the bar. He was dozing off after a steady series of beers that he began putting away when the Inn's opening bell rang at 9 o'clock that morning.

Jersey Jack was in Father Tom's makeshift confessional booth. The two of them had been engaged in a serious conversation about the Eagles' futile quest to win a Super Bowl. After about an hour, their focus had shifted to Jack's belief that if Jesus had been a delivery cart driver, Jack and his Teamster brothers would receive more respect and earn a better hourly wage than union carpenters.

"It's all public relations. See, it's pretty simple, really. I'm talkin' appearances here, ya followin' me, padre?" Jersey Jack was overheard asking the priest. "Ya look at all those fancy TV commercials," he stressed. "Them guys with their new hammers and power saws, they're always thin, good lookin'. Their work clothes are always spotless clean, with nice straight creases in their pants. Got new pickups that look like they ain't never been used. But us truck drivers, on the other hand, we all look about 80 pounds overweight, with beer guts and dirty shirts all covered with oil. We gotta three-day beard and are in a miserable freakin' mood. Our trucks look like crap, ain't been washed in months. With piles of wrappers and beer cans rolling around in the cab."

"And you say," Father Tom replied, "that's because . . . ."

"Because JC, Jesus Christ, plus his old man, Saint Joseph, was in *their* union, the damn carpenters' union. And till the end of freakin' time, your dependable, hard-workin', ball-bustin' truck driver is gonna be misunderstood. Looked on like a lower-class worker. With no chance in hell of movin' ahead and gettin' a top-level, decent-payin' wage."

"But if Jesus had been a delivery person," Father Tom replied, slowly, stringing Jack along, already guessing where the conversation was heading.

"RIGHT!" Jersey Jack said, excitedly. "If you seen pictures of Him drivin' a two-wheeled wagon, with a friendly mule, deliverin' wine and droppin' stuff off to folks, like them shepherd friends of His, out in the fields. Why, that woulda made them smile, and JC woulda represented us as a friend to all. Then we'd be better appreciated. But, that's not how it turned out at all. See, padre, all of this stuff is what the experts call *subliminational*. That hasta do with this continuous series of secret messages bein' sent over the airwaves in your advertisin'. Understand?"

Smiling, the priest picked up his beer, covered his grin and replied, "You may have something there, Jack. I never thought of it in quite that way. That is very perceptive of you. Very deep."

Pleased he possibly had lured a convert into his fold, Jersey Jack raised his glass and toasted both the priest's savvy and his own skillful powers of persuasion.

The stranger, who had overheard the exchange from his stool at the bar, smiled at Joey. Then the man leaned back slightly and pulled an article out of his overcoat pocket. With some care, he pressed the folded paper flat against the smooth surface of the bar.

"Do you believe in miracles?" the stranger asked as he looked up at Joey.

Startled and immediately feeling uneasy, Joey began to head toward Long John at the other end of the bar. As he began stepping away, Joey shouted back, "Look, I gotta go and check on . . . ."

"Please, listen to me," the stranger shouted. "I just want to hang out a bit, talk a little bit. Okay?" Catching Joey's eyes, he held out a piece of paper. "Look at this magazine article. I've been carrying it around for two months." He pressed it onto the bar's flat surface. His finger pointed to the top of the page, near the headline stating: "Who Says Miracles Aren't Real? Extremely High Percentage of Top Docs Believe in Miracles!"

"Look here, pal. It says nearly 75 percent of doctors believe that miracles have happened in the past, and also that 73 percent of them believe miracles can happen today, in the 21st century. What do you think of that?"

"I don't know. It's a high percentage, I guess."

"You guess? What are you, blind? Or are you slow or something?" The guy's tone had turned confrontational, as if he was trying to start an argument. "Can't you count? This article says three out of four doctors think miracles have occurred. And all of these guys are professionals. Educated. So what about that, huh, pal?"

Joey looked across the bar. Occasionally, he had come upon annoying customers looking for a fight. Long ago he had learned the best thing to do was agree with whatever they said.

"So?" the dresser pressed, "I said, what to you think about that, pal?"

Joey clenched his hands, which were hidden below the bar towel, into two tight fists. Then he forced himself to offer a big smile while thinking, *How about this, pal? I'd like to grab your ugly skinny neck and . . . .*

"And choke me until I begged you to stop? Is that what you want to do, Joey?"

The familiarity of the high-pitched voice registered immediately and Joey involuntarily shook his head. "Izzy!" Joey said, his eyes widening and his face creating a toothpaste commercial smile.

"Don't Izzy me, you dunce!" The customer's face was a definite frown. "Because of you I had to come back to this godforsaken city and track you down. They want me to talk some sense into you, put you back on the path."

Joey looked from side to side and leaned forward. "Whadaya talkin' about, Izzy. I've been doing good. And who's *they* anyway?" Then Joey paused and wondered aloud. "Haven't I been doing good?"

"Listen, Joey, if I am here, it is not because I was told to present you with the Keepers' Outstanding Achievement Award. They—the big shots upstairs, where I happen to live now—are concerned that, in certain ways, you are taking your responsibilities too lightly."

"What the hell's that supposed to mean?" Joey made no effort to hide his annoyance.

"Let me explain." Izzy said, then paused and rolled his eyes. "The situation with the textile mill, that raised some eyebrows upstairs, Joey. That and several other incidents that all seem to related to what we call 'checkbook jobs.' In other words, you are distributing money, but you are not investing any personal stake in your work. You are taking the easy way out, Joey. You have got to start to perform more good works using the special skills you have been given—these are the hidden talents that also will take a personal toll, a substantial investment of your strength and judgment. Do you understand what I am talking about?"

Joey leaned forward, pointed to the paper and said, "They want miracles, right?"

"That is precisely what I am trying to say," Izzy said, nodding and tapping on the news clipping.

Joey didn't reply.

After a few seconds of silence, Izzy said, "I know you're concerned about whether you'll pick the right people, if what you try to do will be successful. Your apprehension, your hesitancy, is natural. It is to be expected at this early stage. But, Joey, you must begin to expand your use of your talents. Do you understand?"

Slightly annoyed at Izzy's criticism, the bartender nodded.

"Good," Izzy said, patting Joey on his forearm. He then asked, "So, my young friend, tell me, do you enjoy the work?"

Joey relaxed and nodded. "It's great, and there's always more to do. My mind is always running at top speed, thinking of new ways to find people who need what we can offer. Last week, I went into church, after the Mass was over, and I read through the Book of

Intentions. Izzy, there are so many people who need help—and this is only in one small church.

"One woman wanted a better job for her husband. Another was begging for a liver transplant. People were asking for help on how to have faith and hope, to believe in the future. Several had written they had given up; others pleaded for some sign or any kind of guidance. There were some who asked for money for heat and food. Someone else wanted to settle a family quarrel. There's so much pain in those pages. So many people in need."

Izzy smiled and said, "These are the people whose ills cannot be cured by money, Joey. They need what you can give."

"You're right, Izzy. I know that. I guess I always knew that, but there's no one but you I can talk to. No one else can help me. I've tried to pray for guidance. And sometimes I think, if my wife only knew what I was doing . . . . " Then Joey ended with a forced chuckle.

Looking serious, Izzy replied, "Do not deceive yourself, my young friend. The women know much more than they allow us to realize. And that is the truth, not conjecture."

"How?" Joey asked.

"If I knew the answer to that, Joey, I would have become a marriage counselor rather than a baker and a jeweler."

The men paused and let the conversation lapse. Their discussion turned toward Joey's family situation.

He told Izzy how well his son's studies were progressing and how good it was to have him living at home throughout the year, and attending the local school.

"Just one of the benefits of your good work," Izzy said. "And your Janice has done well, helping improve the school closer to your home. You have the money. It is good you are using it to improve conditions for your son and his friends."

"Thanks, Izzy. You know that's the one thing that bothers me a lot," Joey said. "Not being able to help my son. It's very hard for me to be generous and have the power to lend a hand to strangers but not take care of my own."

Reaching across the bar and pressing his hand down on Joey's arm, Izzy said, "Nothing is perfect in this life, not even for the Keepers, Joey. You'll just have to do the best you can for him, your wife—even strangers who come in here, like me."

Excited to share more personal information, Joey added that JJ, who had been studying at home for several months, spent the last week in Pittsburgh, at his former deaf school, visiting his friends and performing in a play.

"Janice is flying out today, to pick him up," Joey said. "Imagine, she tried to argue with me when I told her to book a first-class ticket. So when she wouldn't do it, I called and did it myself. Both ways. She might as well travel in style, right Izzy?"

"Of course," the mentor replied. "Only the best for our special ladies."

Joey smiled and Izzy stood up from the stool, abruptly ending their reunion. "I've got to be going," he said, offering a weak salute.

"Whadaya have an appointment?"

"As a matter of fact, something rather pressing just came up." Izzy said, looking at his watch. "Besides, your regulars will be wondering about us. I'm sure you'll be able to create a good cover story as soon as I'm gone."

"So we'll meet again, Izzy?" Joey asked.

Izzy shook his head. "Who knows, my young friend. It is possible."

"I'll shift gears, Izzy. I won't let you down. You'll see. I'll do what you suggested, work on the other talents you've given me. I'll make you proud."

Shaking his head, Izzy smiled, then added, "You are doing a very good job, Joey. I have no complaints. I just came to offer some suggestions, provide a small amount of support."

"So that's why you came? To tell me that?"

Izzy nodded. "That and to remind you to have faith, Joey. Good things will come of what you are doing. But not everything seems to be for the best. Your life will not be smooth. There will be things even you, as the Keeper, cannot control or fix. When that happens, don't despair. It is all for a reason, Joey. Trust me."

A sudden flash of fear swept through Joey's body. It was searing hot, like a flame igniting his veins.

"What are you talking about, Izzy?" he said, trying to get the man's attention. But the stranger had already stepped off the barstool, had turned to walk away.

"Come back, Izzy, STOP!" Joey shouted. But the stranger continued walking out of the bar. Joey ran through the narrow counter opening and grabbed him by the arm.

"Let go, pal!" the stranger shouted. The voice was different, harsh, someone else's. Izzy was gone, and the stranger was yanking his arm away from Joey's grasp.

Jersey Jack and Father Tom had left their booth and were moving toward the commotion.

"What did you mean, Izzy?" Joey repeated.

"Name's not Izzy, pal," the man snapped. "And if you got a problem, we can take it outside, right now. How about it?"

Joey stood still. He realized it was too late. The meeting was over. He mumbled an apology as he turned and walked away from the door. The stranger exited, but he had left the medical miracles article on the counter. Joey folded the clipping and shoved it into his pants pocket.

Jersey Jack and Father Tom headed back to their booth. Long John was still out for the count. He hadn't seen or heard a thing.

For the next few hours, Joey tried to figure out the real reason for Izzy's surprise visit. Was there any meaning or message in Izzy's short conversation? Joey knew he would find out eventually, but he had a horrible feeling that there was no miracle he could perform that would stop whatever tragedies had been predestined to occur.

CHAPTER 20
Fire in the Sky

The 4 o'clock, late afternoon rush was starting to peak. Joey had his hands full with the usual after-work crowd. Knowing what most of them drank made it easier to cope with their needs, but for a solid 40 minutes it was a steady routine of passing drinks across the bar and responding to requests for refills.

FoxNews was on the TV in the poolroom. The other set hanging above the bar was tuned to the same station, but set to mute. Bold words set against a narrow black rectangular box crawled continually across the bottom of the screen.

Long ago, the regulars had voted that the bar set be placed on mute, so the volume wouldn't interfere with their arguments and antics. Those interested in hearing the news could sit beside the set in the poolroom or read the latest announcements as they appeared.

If it wasn't for Long John, who awakened after a five-hour nap, Joey would not have known about the plane crash at the western end of the state.

"Damn!" the regular shouted. "Look at that crash in Pittsburgh. Hellava lotta fire comin' outta that plane."

At the mention of the word Pittsburgh, Joey stopped moving and jerked his head toward the television. Dropping a full bottle of beer, he ran to the back counter, grabbed the remote and turned up the volume.

"FAA officials are unsure of the cause of the fire. However, one anonymous representative said the explosion took place in the first-class cabin and spread rapidly through the first four rows in the interior of the plane.

"Several passengers were treated for smoke inhalation and there are unconfirmed reports of several deaths, but officials are withholding the names until the next of kin are notified.

"To summarize, PennAirways Flight number 708, from Philadelphia to Pittsburgh, experienced an explosion in the first class

cabin upon landing. At this time there is no evidence of terrorist activity, but several passengers have been injured and there are unconfirmed reports of fatalities. This is Ron Polemous, FoxNews reporting."

Joey grabbed his cell phone and pressed in his wife's number. There was no answer. Either it has been shut off or there was a worse reason she didn't respond.

Nervously, Joey scanned the bar and shouted across the room, "JERSEY JACK, LONG JOHN! Take over. I gotta get to Pittsburgh. Janice was on that flight."

Heading out the door, he shouted. "I'll call Uncle Lou from my car. You guys cover the bar until he comes in."

"No problem," they said as the Inn's door slammed, and Joey disappeared, running into the street.

* * *

Within 45 minutes Henry Staltzmann was able to charter a plane to fly Joey to Pittsburgh. He said it would be ready to go at a private hanger in the Philadelphia airport complex.

Driving like a madman Joey rushed to the private plane terminal, left his car in the lot and ran toward the waiting corporate jet. Less than two hours after hearing the news, Joey's flight was rolling to a stop at a small airport outside Pittsburgh, not far from the main terminal, which had been closed because of the incident on Flight 708.

During the flight and ride he had called Janice's cell phone more than a dozen times. But she never answered. All he got was an impersonal recorded message, telling him the person he was calling was temporarily unavailable. Joey hoped that was true.

It took him another hour to gain access to the lounge holding the terrified passengers. As bomb squad personnel, FAA inspectors, sky marshals and Homeland Security agents combed the damaged plane, PennAirways personnel responded to calls and visitors seeking information on their loved ones.

During his flight, Joey had called his credit card company and retrieved information about his wife's trip, including her seat number, which would be needed to obtain information.

After showing his identification, and explaining that his wife had been in the first-class section, Joey was allowed to enter the restricted area reserved for relatives seeking news. After waiting less than two minutes, a PennAirways official asked Joey to step into a smaller room. Once inside, two women invited him to sit and, pulling out a diagram of the plane's interior, pointed out the site of the explosion.

The origination point was in seat A-12, directly next to his wife, who was seated in A-11.

The taller woman, dressed in a dark blue uniform, was talking to him, but Joey just heard pieces of her conversation. His malfunctioning mind could only process slivers of remarks, but they made little sense.

"We only have preliminary information at this . . . ."

His head was spinning, his entire body spiraling nearly out of control.

"There are only a few bodies in the restricted area, and we are not sure . . . ."

He felt weak, as if he were going to faint.

"We understand your apprehension, and it would have been wrong on our part not to tell you as much . . . ."

Joey had heard enough. He stood up, unsteadily, beginning to walk toward the larger waiting room.

"We'll be in touch the moment we know any . . . ."

He felt a hand guiding him out to wait with the other troubled souls, all hoping for the best. Some were praying intently with their eyes closed. Joey could read their lips. He recognized the soft, pleading recitations of *Hail Mary's* and *Glory Be's*.

Joey looked at his watch, but he could not read the dial. He recognized the numbers but he was unable to translate them into time. Instead he thought of what Izzy had said that very day—how he, Joey, with all his power, could not control everything. That he was not immune to pain and suffering. That he and his loved ones were at risk as much as the poorest persons on earth. And already his mentor's prediction had come true.

Or, Joey thought, *or did he know something? Did Izzy know this was going to happen? Did he appear today to prepare me for the tragedy? But if he knew in advance, why the hell didn't Izzy tell me, so I could call Janice? Make her stay home, or take a different plane. Keep her safe?*

Joey's sadness turned to boiling rage. Anger overwhelmed him. He cursed Izzy, God, the damned coins that started this all. And while he saw how much they allowed him to do, their power was useless when it came to his affecting own life, and those closest to the damned Keeper himself. He had a limitless supply of money at his fingertips. He could change the fortunes of people he had never met. But for his wife and son, the treasures of his life, their safety and their welfare were beyond his reach.

Lowering his head into his hands, Joey began to sob. He tried to contain his feelings but the pain was too severe. Looking around, he raced through a restroom door in the corner. Charging inside he flipped the latch, fell to the floor and began to cry. The emotional release was so intense that his chest ached and his throat became raw. He didn't know how long he had remained in the room. At some point he must have fallen asleep, for the sound of a latch opening the door awakened him.

A guard, who had used his master key, poked his head in the door and allowed another man to enter the restroom. The poor soul apparently had received similar bad news. Joey got up, brushed off the back of his pants and walked unsteadily toward the sink.

He felt no embarrassment. He was too consumed by the loss of his wife. Images of wasted time spent fighting over stupid issues passed trough his mind. *To have those precious moments back,* he thought, *there isn't any price I wouldn't pay.*

As he exited the bathroom, he headed for a seat in the waiting area, somewhere far away from the other mourners. He needed to think about what to do next, how to break the news to JJ. How to deal with their future, without the most important person in his life.

Signaling with a weak wave that he wanted privacy to anyone that might think of approaching him, Joey closed his eyes and tried to think, to organize. In the darkness of his mind, Janice's beautiful face smiled at him, trying to tell him everything would be fine, that he would be able to move on.

But it wasn't a person that interfered with his solitude, it was his cell phone. The vibrating motion distracted him from his thoughts and, although he wanted to avoid talking to anyone, he instinctively pulled the device from his pocket.

Perhaps it's some news about Janice, or JJ, he thought. *Damn*, he suddenly remembered, *I should have called the school to alert them that we, I, would be late in picking up my son.*

"Yes!" he snapped, irritated with the interruption.

"Joey?"

It was Janice.

Joey was stunned. At first he thought he had pushed the message button and he was listening to a saved recording. He pulled the phone away from his face to check the caller ID, but he didn't recognize the number.

"JOEY? JOEY? ARE YOU THERE?" the voice shouted. "It's me, Janice. JOEY?"

Gasping and unable to respond calmly, he forced a deep breath and replied. "Jan. Jan, I'm here. In Pittsburgh. Where are you?"

"At the school. I had to get here to calm down JJ. They heard about the crash and he thought I was injured or dead. He was going out of control. As soon as they allowed me to leave the airport, I raced out here and picked him up.

"I would have called you, but I lost my cell phone, probably somewhere on the plane. During the crash. I'm sorry I didn't get to you sooner, but it was horrible. I was so worried about JJ."

Joey let her know he was fine. Everything would be all right. He was happy she was safe. They could talk about it later.

"I called Uncle Lou. He told me you had flown out to the crash. Oh, Joey, I love you. I'm sorry I didn't call sooner. It's been crazy, just getting here and arguing to leave the airport and going to pick up JJ. They weren't going to let me leave."

"Relax, Janice. I'm fine. I'm fine now." Joey paused to control his building emotions. "I thought you were . . . . They said they didn't know anything for sure, here. It's mass confusion."

Janice interjected. "No. I'm fine, perfect. Not even a scratch. It was a miracle, Joey. I swear, it's a miracle I'm still here. Please, just wait there for us. We're at the school now. Just leaving. I'll be at the airport in less than an hour. All right?"

Joey agreed and told them to take their time. He would wait for her, for them, forever, if necessary.

"I love you, Joey."

"I love you, too, Janice. I always will," he replied softly, ending the call.

Then Joey let his head fall back against the seat, tried to let the tension go, and slept very peacefully for what seemed a long time. But it less than an hour he was awakened to see his wife and son, smiling and showering him with kisses and hugs.

* * *

Rather than fly back to Philadelphia that night, Joey and Janice decided to stay in a motel next to the airport. PennAirways provided a room and meals for the entire family, and Janice's survival solved one of the major mysteries associated with the crash.

After JJ was asleep on the cot at the foot of their bed, Janice explained how she had lived through the explosion. And Joey listened very closely to her story.

"I was in the boarding area, waiting to go onto the plane. That's when I saw a young man, a soldier, sitting by himself. He had a pleasant face but looked a bit apprehensive. Now I know you had gotten the first-class seat, and I felt uncomfortable spending all that money on myself. So . . ."

"So you gave him your seat," Joey said.

Shaking her head, Janice added, "Not right away. It wasn't until I was on that plane and we were in the air. I was walking toward the restroom and passed him. He had an aisle seat, toward the rear of the plane, and he was straining across two overly sized people to get a view out the window. So I stopped and talked with him."

Janice found out the boy was from Ohio and heading home. He had never been on a commercial flight. Impulsively, she took him by the hand and told him she had a better view in her seat and she wanted him to have it.

"He tried to decline, but I wouldn't hear of it. I pulled him to the front of the plane. Everyone was clapping and cheering as he headed for first class. The attendant tried to tell me I wasn't allowed to switch seats in flight, but I ignored her. I told her he was a fighting man and deserved to get the best. He gave me a hug and that was the last I saw him.

"But I remember his name. Flowers, Isaac Flowers. I thought it was a strange, old-fashioned name for a strong, good looking boy. He must have had his share of problems and teasing about it while he was growing up."

Joey continued to listen to Janice's story. She was wired, in no mood to go to sleep.

She said the explosion went off as they were nearing the airport. The plane rocked and smoke started pouring out of the first-class section of the plane. It was some time before she realized that the area where she had been sitting had been the section that was damaged.

Janice said she wanted to get information, about the injuries, about what happened, who may have been hurt. But in the confusion the attendants were concentrating all their efforts on keeping the passengers calm and in their seats.

"As they landed, we raced off the plane and were pulled into groups by airline and customs officials. They were verifying our identities, checking our clothing. They were checking for terrorist accomplices, a whole range of possibilities. I never saw Private Flowers leave the plane. I hoped he was all right. I don't know who was hurt, who was killed. All we got were rumors. They gave us no information at all."

After about an hour, Janice said she was released and able to head for JJ's school. Eventually, she called Joey and that was all she knew.

She said she explained the seat switch with Private Flowers to authorities, but they looked at her like she was crazy. They said she had been in her seat and that there was no Private Isaac Flowers on the passenger list.

"I swear it happened," Janice said. "I remember people cheering as that young man walked into first class. I did not sit in my seat on the plane. I sat in his, near the back."

"I know," Joey said. "I believe you. I saw a diagram of the site where the explosion occurred. It was the seat next to yours. If you were there, you would have been killed."

"So who was there, Joey. Who was in my seat? Who was my miracle man?"

"I don't know, Jan. We'll probably never know. But all we can do is be thankful we're still together. Take advantage of this precious gift of extra time."

As Joey looked down, his wife had finally fallen asleep in the overstuffed chair. He lifted her body and carried her into bed, pulling the covers up to her neck. She was so peaceful, breathing deeply. So very much alive.

He walked into the bathroom, pulled his trousers off. As he was hanging them on a hook, he felt something in the right pocket. He reached inside. It was the magazine article about doctors and their belief in miracles that Izzy had left on the bar. Carefully, Joey unfolded the papers and flipped the pages. At the bottom of the last page, on the back, was written:

I. Flowers, Pvt. U.S. Army. Do you believe in miracles?

Joey nodded, looked up and whispered, "Thank you, Private I. Flowers. Thank you, Mister I. Bloom."

CHAPTER 21
Thanksgiving Dinner

The Novaks shared Thanksgiving dinner with Uncle Lou, along with Long John and Father Tom, who had nowhere to go. It was nice for JJ to spend some time with his larger, adopted, extended family. Father Tom said grace, and after dinner Long John told JJ stories of the old man's exploits as a merchant seaman and treasure hunter. JJ had advanced quite well at reading lips, but Long John took care to face the boy while telling his tall tales.

While Janice and Joey were in the kitchen, cleaning dishes and cooking pots, Uncle Lou came in to thank them again for the meal and to talk a bit before heading out. Father Tom was with him, and the two men each grabbed a chair.

"Real shame about Donna and the diner," Lou said, lifting the handle of his coffee cup. Father Tom nodded and shrugged his shoulders.

"What are you talking about?" Joey asked.

"A developer is doin' some serious lookin' to buy the South Street Diner. Old Man Lukosh could be makin' a bundle. It's closin' at the end of the year. Donna and the girls will be outta work with slim prospects for findin' another job very easy."

"Some Merry Christmas bonus," Father Tom said weakly.

"That's impossible," Janice said. "Business is always good. You can hardly ever get a seat. Margie and I were in there last week, at 10 o'clock, after the morning rush. It was still jammed. You can't tell me Lukosh needs the money."

"He's old," Uncle Lou said. "Just like me. He can't keep up with the place. But he don't have no good lookin' nephew like Joey here to help out. He told me he wants to go to Florida and can't find a buyer to take over the business, so he's talkin' to the developer. And he'd be crazy not to."

"If he could, he'd sell it to somebody who would keep the place going," Father Tom said. "No one, not even Old Man Lukosh, would be pleased to see his life's work turned into another strip mall."

"So the issue must be money, right?" Janice said, tossing the dish towel on the counter beside the sink. Her face a sudden scowl.

"Give the lovely little lady a stuffed elephant!" Uncle Lou said, laughing. "According to what I hear, the developer offered Lukosh an even mill. But he says if he could find somebody in the area to keep the business goin', he'd let 'em have it for half that price. He'd love to have the place go on, like a personal tribute to him after he moves to the Orange State. But he says he's gotta get a decent price for it. And, nobody's come knockin' on his door with any good offers. So let's be honest, that kinda money just ain't floatin' around the neighborhood."

"What about the girls?" Joey asked.

Uncle Lou almost coughed up his coffee. "Yeah, right! Donna and her girlfriends in charge of the place. That would be a laugh."

"And why's that?" snapped Janice in a tone conveying her perceived insult. As the men meekly turned to face the woman of the house, she added, "Who knows better than those ladies how to run that place? Old Man Lukosh just sits at the register on his fat dupa and does as little as possible. It's Donna, Irene, Lakesha, Sophia and Angela who do all the work and have developed the clientele."

Father Tom raised a hand, attempting to interject a note of sanity, but Janice gave the priest a cold stare and she kept on going. "Even when Ben the Cook doesn't show up half the time on Sunday mornings, 'cause he's sleeping off a hangover, the girls cover the kitchen for him. And they do a damn good job at it. They could run that place and turn a tidy profit. I swear, you men won't give them the least bit of credit."

Janice turned away and began mumbling to herself while scrubbing a dirty pot and slamming it against the side of the sink.

Joey glanced around the table, feeling he had to say something to break the mood. "Look, Jan. We were only joking. Of course, Donna and the girls could do a good job. Right Uncle Lou? Father Tom?"

Fearing another barrage of abuse from the little woman, the two male guests would have agreed to the beatification of Paris Hilton. Together they added their enthusiastic agreement to Joey's comment.

Turning, Janice leaned back against the sink counter and faced them. Annoyed, she decided to press her agenda further. "Good. Uncle Lou. You know Donna's number. Get her on the phone."

As he slowly walked toward the kitchen wall phone, Lou turned and meekly asked, "Why?"

"So I can see if she wants to buy the place with me and take over the job as full-time manager."

Realizing it was best not to question his niece when her eyes looked like flaming coals, the owner of the Welcome Inn got the waitress on the phone and passed the receiver to Jan.

After a 20-minute conversation, while pacing around in the dining room, Janice returned, hung up the phone and said. "It's settled. Tomorrow Joey will meet with Old Man Lukosh and his attorney. I'm going to invest my inheritance in the place and will own 70 percent of the diner. Donna and the girls will come up with the rest. If not, we'll find a way to cover it. That's it."

Smiling at the confusion etched on the men's faces, Janice turned on her charm and in a lilting voice asked, "Now, would anyone like more coffee?"

Uncle Lou and Father Tom smiled and nodded, afraid to refuse. As their guests sat at the kitchen table and discussed the amazing developments, Joey pulled his wife into the corner of the dining room.

"Do you know what you're doing?" Joey whispered, his voice less than friendly.

"Perfectly well," Janice said, looking her husband in the eye.

"We can't just spend more than a quarter million dollars like that," he whispered.

Janice looked into his eyes and whispered, "Oh yes we can, Joey. You do it almost every day."

"What are you talking about?"

"Let's not go there, Joey Novak. Let's just leave it at that. I made a decision. Now you can make it happen. Just call your new best friend, Mr. Henry Staltzmann, who owns half of center city, and tell him to do it. Isn't that how your game works, Joey?"

Her shocked husband didn't respond, didn't know what to say. In the end, he decided to say nothing. He wanted to get through the surprising encounter without opening a discussion that might lead to places he didn't want to go.

"Fine," he said, and turned to return to the kitchen and the safety of his guests.

"But you remember this, Joey Novak," Janice said, "I know more about your work and association with *Mr. Isadore Bloomwitz* of the *Polish Consulate* than you think."

Shaking his head, Joey didn't reply. But he recalled Izzy's comment a few weeks earlier in the Welcome Inn: *Do not deceive yourself, my young friend. The women know much more than they allow us to realize. And that is the truth, not conjecture.*

Chapter 22

Exception to the Rule

It was 2 o'clock in the morning, early on the Friday after Thanksgiving. In Philadelphia, like everywhere else during the holiday weekend, the streets were unusually quiet. Several old riverfront warehouses were emptying, as the last of many tired parade workers had just finished putting away decorations and floats that had rolled through Center City Philly during the traditional Thanksgiving Day extravaganza.

Joey couldn't sleep. He left his bed and walked toward the garage. With a small shovel, he dug up the can from the yard containing the Kings' Coins. He knew he had told Izzy they would be placed in a safer place, but he'd been so busy that he had forgotten to get it done. Later in the day, he was going to take them to a bank vault and rent a secure deposit box. When he was settled on the couch in his hideaway above the garage, Joey reached inside the can, removed the blue cloth pouch and gently placed the contents on the clean surface of a low wooden table.

For several minutes, Joey sat back and stared at the relics. To know, he thought, that these small golden pieces of tribute had been touched the by hands of history's most important people—the Christ Child, the Blessed Virgin, St. Joseph, the Crusaders, even Joan of Arc.

And here he was, a nobody, with a high school diploma, who was selected to care for them and use them to perform virtuous deeds, to share their miraculous goodness. During this season of thanks, Joey felt he needed to pause and marvel at the wonder of it all, to gaze upon their power one more time.

There was no denying the tremendous good that had happened to him—and to others—since he had assumed the Keeper's role.

Now he had to move them to a safer place, where they were secure from accidental discovery or theft. With them, too, he would place a letter, his statement, that would direct the next Keeper to come to him when the time came.

Of course, there was no hurry, and Izzy had explained that the letter could be updated as needed. But Joey, using his mentor's message as a guide, had typed his own instructions.

In the dim light of his private place, Joey, the Keeper, read it once more.

Hello:

We're living in a dangerous time, filled with unimaginable threats of terror. But it's also a time when the world is filled with more good people than bad. For many years, I've been honored to care for these special coins.

To keep them safe, I placed them in this vault. If you have opened it and are reading this letter, then you've come into possession of the key and opened the special box. And that wasn't by accident.

I've been waiting for you. I know you're reading this note and wondering if this is some kind of joke. And, I'm sure you are asking: Why me?

You're also wondering if you should follow these instructions or toss them aside and sell the gold coins. I'm sure you know you could get some serious money for them.

I had the same questions years ago, when I found myself in your exact situation. But I know you'll follow these instructions because you're curious and, more importantly, because you've been selected—like I also was selected.

And neither of us have any other choice.

You see, you're now the newest Keeper of the Coins, and you are responsible for their care and safety. This isn't an accident. You were selected years ago; however, the exact, time and place of the discovery, and your identity, were unknown. But there was never any doubt the transition process of responsibility and power would eventually occur.

Within 24 hours bring this letter, but not the coins, to me, Joey Novak. I am waiting for you at the Welcome Inn, a corner bar located in the Fishtown section of Philadelphia, Pennsylvania, U.S.A. I'm sure you will find it.

Come alone, between 7 and 8 a.m. Since the bar doesn't open until 9 a.m., ring the bell and I'll let you in. We have a lot to talk about.

Don't bring anyone with you.

From this moment, your life, and your family's lives, have changed in ways you can't imagine. But it's all for the better. I know. I had the same doubts as you do. You will learn that you've been given tremendous responsibilities. I know you're confused, that you think this is crazy. These reactions are normal; in fact, they're expected. Just come to the Inn and I'll fill you in.

Looking forward to our meeting,

Joey Novak
Philadelphia, Pennsylvania
November 26, 2007

Joey stopped reading and placed the typed paper on the table beside the coins. As he began to fold the letter, he looked up. Janice was standing across the room. He hadn't heard her arrive.

"Did you finish your letter?" she asked.

Startled, Joey smiled and asked, "How long have you known?"

"A little while," she said, taking a seat on the tattered couch beside her husband.

"But how?" Joey was surprised. He thought he had kept his secret life from Janice.

"Oh, Joey! I noticed how you've changed, how you read the smallest items in the paper, how you take notes while we're watching the news. You make whispered calls at all hours to your accountant friend. I was up here one day and you left out a long list of all the children's hospitals within a hundred miles. I just kept quiet and listened."

He shook his head. "I wasn't allowed to tell you. I made a serious promise."

She smiled at him. "To Izzy. I know. He came to visit me a few days after the plane crash. He filled me in so I wouldn't go crazy, trying to figure out the unexplained events and the appearance of my phantom soldier. He also told me about how he had been troubled for years that he could do nothing to save the countess, his first love. So maybe, Joey, Izzy didn't want you to suffer the way he's had to, all these years."

Janice paused, waiting for Joey to respond. When her husband remained silent, she said, "I understand now why you kept things from me. It's okay. And while I don't know everything, or the specifics of how things work, I know that you're doing good, Joey. That you're helping people—forgotten, needy people. That's what's important." Looking directly at the gold coins resting on the table, she said, "They're beautiful. You must be so very honored."

Looking into her eyes, Joey smiled and a tear fell onto his cheek.

"No. No. Joey. No tears. Please."

"You don't understand," he said. "I'm going to be doing this for a very, very long time. Long after . . . "

"Long after JJ and I are gone. I know," she said, pulling him close. "Long after other loves and countless friends and people I will never meet will pass through your life, Joey."

He held her back at arms length and looked at his beautiful wife. Not knowing what to say.

"But you know what, Joey Novak," Janice said. "I am your first love. I'll always be your first love, no matter what happens after I'm gone. That means I'll be the first woman in line waiting for you when you pass through those Pearly Gates. You'll see me and JJ and even Isadore Bloom, hand in hand, rushing toward you, Joey. And you and I will start our love affair all over again. How does that sound?"

"Great," Joey said, holding her and shaking as he tried to stifle the aching pain surrounding his heart.

Janice wrapped her arms around her trembling husband and pulled him close. With her lips next to his ear she said, "Izzy saved me, Joey. He prolonged my life on that plane. And that was for a reason, a very important reason. I want to have another baby, Joey. I want another child with you, my love."

Holding her tightly, Joey nodded as he cried with joy. For so many years they had been hesitant, afraid to try again. But now their fear didn't matter. They tossed their inhibitions and concerns aside, and gave into desperate love and the purest of passion. And during Thanksgiving weekend, on a secondhand couch in Joey's hideaway above the garage, the caring couple shared their deepest love.

Unnoticed by the lovers as they joined, creating their miracle child, the Kings' Coins glowed slightly brighter beside them throughout the night.

CHAPTER 23
'Seven Then Heaven'

Only three weeks remained before Christmas arrived and Joey was in full swing. After Thanksgiving weekend, Janice had taken an active role, helping her husband sort out the most deserving among the multitudes of needy.

JJ was upstairs, getting ready for the arrival of his tutor. At the kitchen table, Janice shoved a newspaper article she has circled toward her husband.

"Look at this, Joey. Why not do it here? Wouldn't that be great?"

The small headline read: "Donation of gold coins a mystery"

Salvation Army officials don't know who has been dropping gold coins into their Christmas kettles over the past several years, but officials said they hope the mysterious donations continue.

More than 200 gold coins have been discovered since the early 1990s. Each has an average value of more than $300 and that figure varies based on current prices of the valuable commodity.

South African Kruggerands, as well as U.S., German, Chinese and Canadian coins have been among those donated to the non-profit organization.

National Salvation Army spokesperson Major Leland Junt said, 'We have found gold coins in New York City, Los Angeles, Baltimore and Miami. But they even have shown up in smaller cities, including Peoria, Ill., Fenwick Island, Del., Fayetteville, N. C., and Shamokin, Pa. Certainly, we accept all forms of currency and are not particular,' Junt said, with a smile, 'but if people want to give us gold, like the Three Kings gave the Christ Child, we'll be happy to accept it and we will use the precious gifts to spread goodwill to all.'

Joey finished reading and set down the paper. When he didn't say anything, Janice pressed him for an answer.

"No!" he said, firmly.

"Why not?" she asked, annoyed at his negative response.

"Because," he said.

"That's not an answer."

"Yes it is an answer, but maybe not good enough for you."

"So offer a better one, other than 'I'm the Keeper and I have the final say!' " Janice said in a mocking tone.

Lowering his coffee cup firmly against the tabletop, Joey waited for the clack to resound and snapped at his wife. "Because this is not a game. And because if you do this kinda stunt in large quantities, in the same place, it would call attention to our area. And that we don't need."

"I don't understand," Janice said, her voice calm and displaying sincere interest in his explanation.

"Look, Jan," he said, "Izzy hid the coins to keep them out of the hands of the Nazis. He implied there are people out there who would be seriously interested in obtaining them, and with the intent to use the power for no good, or they'd sell them with no understanding of their true importance and mystical value. So, it's best we try to keep a low profile about their existence and whereabouts. Dropping gold coins in red buckets in the Delaware Valley would attract too much attention, and, as I said, we don't need it."

After a brief moment of silence, Jan assured Joey she understood and agreed. Then, with a lilt in her voice, she asked, "Then I'll compromise, assuming you don't have a problem if I drop a $100 bill with Mr. Ben Franklin's picture on it in a few kettles here and there?"

Lifting the paper in front of his face, Joey mumbled, "And if I said 'No' would it stop you?"

Laughing, Janice raced around the table, gave her husband a hug, and ran upstairs to check on JJ.

* * *

Late that night, Janice was reading in the living room when Joey returned at 10 p.m. from work. Uncle Lou had arrived at the Inn unexpectedly to close up, sending his nephew home early.

Glancing up from her book, Janice noticed her husband's slumped shoulders. His frown was more pronounced, and he offered nothing more than a soft, "How ya doin?"

Knowing how to react to his down-and-out moods, Janice waited about five minutes. She had learned if Joey hadn't opened up by that length of silence, she was going to have to pry the concerns out of him.

When the appropriate moments had passed, she started with "Tough day in the saloon?"

No reply.

After counting to twenty, Janice followed up with, "I hit the Powerball tonight. We're doubly rich now!"

"Funny, Jan. Real funny," he said, calling out softly from a chair in the adjacent kitchen.

Walking in and stopping behind Joey, who had opened a long neck beer, Janice stood and rubbed his neck and shoulders, trying to help him relax. "Talk to me, Joey. Come on. We were sitting here laughing this morning, Everything was right with the world, and now why so glum? What's the matter?"

He shook his head, adding an almost expected, "You won't understand."

Janice stopped the massage, walked away and took a seat directly across the table. "Yes, I will, Joey, or at least I'll try. And I've always been a good listener. Talk to me."

Lifting his head and meeting her eyes, Joey thought for moment, then said, "It's such a pain, Jan."

"What's a pain? What you do mean?" She was sitting beside him, pulling on his hand and trying to draw him closer, urging him to share his thoughts.

Usually, in a situation like this, Joey would engage in a little game of give-and-take and toss silly banter back and forth. But this time he was trapped in the bowels of a landfill. Eventually, he began to voice his frustration with his new lifetime occupation.

"I feel like I'm at the bottom of a broken dam. The water is rushing all over and around me, and I'm trying to stop from being knocked over. And I'm standing there, wobbling, holding this bucket, trying to catch what I can. But no matter how much I get into the bucket, Jan, there's all the rest that's rushing by, all around me. And I can't catch the right stuff. I'm trying to do a job that can't be done."

"So you're saying," she cut in, "that you can only save a small percentage, only help a few. Is that it, Joey?"

He shook his head fiercely, stood up from the table and walked to the back door and stared out its window. "That's part of it, Jan, that I can't do enough. But the other part is: How do I know that I'm picking the right ones? What if I'm missing the ones who need my help more?"

It was listening time, and Janice knew when to remain silent and let the long pauses work their own magic that would cause Joey to fill the dead space with more information.

"I mean, it was nice to help Donna and the girls at the diner, Jan. Don't get me wrong, I was with you on that. But was their problem more important than another family's needs somewhere else? I know I'm missing too much. I'm doing things in little dribs and drabs. I'm responding. I'm only on the defensive. I've got to be more aggressive, get out more, spend more on the right people. But who in the hell and where in the hell are they?"

Before his wife could answer, Joey quickly shifted his focus, telling her about meeting Tony Cutrona, a classmate of theirs from high school, a few nights earlier. Tony was a cop. He had a wife and two small daughters, both younger than JJ. And Tony had a lousy detail, assigned to the dangerous north section of the city, having the highest violent crime and murder rate for the last four years.

"He came into the Inn, Jan," Joey said. "I hadn't seen him in six, maybe eight months. I looked up; he was sitting at the bar, just got off his shift. Ordered a beer. And there was this glow, like a bright yellow shadow outlining his whole body.

"It was the first time I saw that, and I must have looked strange, because Tony put out his hand and said, 'Whadidya see, a ghost?' Then he laughed, and I forced a soft laugh to cover up my shock.

"But the minute I shook his hand, it was creepy. I could see a picture, like a movie scene of Tony. He was shot, in his car, under a streetlight, in front of a deli. The time on his dashboard was 2:34. Since it was dark, it had to be in the morning."

Janice listened closely. Joey paused to recall the facts. He was making an effort to get the story straight.

He told her there were two detectives, taking notes, roaming the crime scene. "They were discussing the 'bad luck of the poor guy, who was filling in for another officer who had called out sick.' Apparently, Tony said he needed some overtime and worked a double. He wasn't even supposed to be on duty that night."

"What did you do?" Janice asked.

Joey shrugged, "What could I do, Jan? Pull him aside and say, 'Hey, Tony! I just had this vision that you're going to be shot in the head sometime after midnight when you do a double at an unspecified time in the future.' Do you know how that would sound? He'd think I was drinking all day behind the bar instead of serving the customers. Besides, I have no idea if it will happen next week, next year or tomorrow night. He could say no to the OT one night and then two nights later he still gets a bullet in his brain."

"So you just let him go? Didn't warn him? Didn't do anything?"

Letting a hiss of air escape his tightly pursed lips, Joey paused, tried to be patient and said, "I'm open to suggestions, Jan. Think I should call his wife and tell her to make him come straight home after work, so he won't get murdered? Think that will help, or just worry her to death?"

When she didn't reply, Joey said, "You see? This so-called gift of mine is really a damn curse, especially when you can't do any good with it. And now I'll be watching the news every night or checking the obits every morning, looking for Tony C's picture."

But all this was just leading up to his main story. That afternoon, Joey said he had spent two hours at the Franklin Children's Hospital. He got in by telling the woman at the front desk he was thinking about volunteering.

"They gave me a tour, Janice. This old guy, a retiree who spends four hours there every day, showed me all around. He took me to the seventh floor last. That's where they have the worst cases, mostly terminal—all types of cancer patients, kidney disorders, brain damage. I'm talking little kids, Jan. Only six, eight years old and younger. I mean, they don't even have a chance at life. They're on the way out and they haven't even lived yet."

Joey stopped for a few seconds, the memories of the tour taking a toll on him emotionally. "Here I am, Jan. I'm going to live for God knows how long. We're financially secure. We have a beautiful son. And before today I was so upset he couldn't hear. God, Janice, I'm so thankful that at least he'll be able to live.

"The old guy, Gus, no Gil. His name was Gil. He said nobody other than parents think about the kids of floor seven. 'Seven then Heaven' they call it. Isn't that pathetic?

"The nurses and doctors who work there, they go through hell every day, seeing these poor little kids, and trying to work miracles." Joey laughed, but it was almost sinister, mocking. "At that moment, I thought, Why me? Why the hell didn't whoever it was give the damn coins to someone who could do something with the power? Why not a doctor, or a researcher? Or even a bishop or world leader? They could use it better than me, Jan. I don't know what the hell I'm doing. I can't help these kids, can't warn Tony C." Then Joey stopped talking and looked at his wife. "So you see why I'm fried?"

Walking toward him and wrapping her arms around his waist, Jan said, "Yeah. I hear what you say. But you have to think, Joey. You can't save the world, not even a small part of it. If you try to do too much you'll go nuts, land up in a crazy house. Then who will take care of things?"

Janice took a quick breath and continued. It was her turn to talk, her time to set things right, give her husband support. He had done it for her, initially, when JJ was born. Now it was her chance to push a heavy dose of reason into his fragile, confused mind, show him how well he had been doing, how much good he had done.

"Have you gone over your journal lately, Joey? Well I did, and you've accomplished a lot in a short time. It's only been a few months and you've saved and changed lives, brought relief and hope to several hundred people. You have to understand, you CANNOT DO IT ALL!" Janice grabbed Joey's face in her hands, "but you can do the best you can. And from what I've seen, you have done just that. And that's why they picked you. Because you're a good, honest, caring man."

Joey took a breath, then offered a weak smile. He was looking for her perspective, her support. It helped a lot. He told her that her opinion was important to him. Then he said, "There was this one moment, Jan, when I was walking down the corridor, and I wanted to go into every room and touch each injured child, try to heal them, mend them, like one of those Bible-thumping preachers on late night TV—but with no jumping around, no stage lights and flash.

"I'm embarrassed to talk about it now, to think I was almost god-like, thought I had all this power. But I wanted to be able to do it, to fix them. Then I realized I couldn't, that I couldn't make that happen. The coins seem to allow me to do the impossible in an individual instance. But when I think large scale, public displays, that's not what the coins are all about, and that kind of stunt, or grandstanding wouldn't be right. I actually heard a voice in my mind tell me if I tried to do something that attracted publicity I'd end up in a white wrap-around coat, strapped down in the back of an ambulance. So I'm confused with what I can and can't do, how much I need to get done. Some of these days it's been a real messed up cluster is all I can say."

"Then you do your best," Janice said, calmly. "And if Izzy or Henry or any of the unknown power figures can do better, or want you to do things differently, they can just show up and tell you." At that point, her tone shifted and she became more firm and directing, "Until that happens, you just keep going along and doing what you want. What YOU want, Joey, not anyone else. You're the one on the front line, making the decisions. You're your own toughest critic because you really care. If someone doesn't like it, then tell them to go to hell!"

They were both silent a moment, then Janice added, "When I was a little girl," she said, "my grandmother gave me her most beautiful necklace, Joey. I remember that moment to this day, even though it was so many years ago. I was absolutely thrilled, because it was my favorite piece of jewelry. And you know what she said to me, with a beaming smile on her face?"

Joey shook his head.

"She said, 'I give this to you with a warm hand, Janice, not a cold hand. So I can see the beautiful, happy smile on your face. If you learned you would have it after I am gone, what joy would I have? Always remember, Janice, to give with a warm hand is better than to give with a cold one.'

"You see, Joey. You have been given the gift of sharing with a warm hand. And rather than worry about what you can't get done, or can't fix, you should be thankful and enjoy the results of your good deeds that you have been blessed to witness."

Joey smiled for the first time since leaving the hospital and, hugging his wife, he let out a tired sigh.

"So what about Tony C?" she asked.

Groaning, Joey said, "I'm thinking hard on that one, trying to figure something out. Maybe I'll send an anonymous threat or warning to the desk sergeant."

Smiling, Janice then asked in her knowing voice, "And how much are you sending the hospital?"

"Who?" Joey replied, his nervous, one-word question was at an unusually high pitch.

"The children's hospital, or course. I'm not an idiot, Joey. How much money are they getting?"

"Well," he said, "I've been spending a lot lately, so Henry thought I should be reasonable. So he's donating a half million now and pledging two million sometime next year."

"That's nice," she said. "What will they use it for?"

"Lots of good things," Joey said. "All kinds of medical stuff. But you'll find out more at the dedication."

"Dedication?"

"Yeah," he said, smiling. "It'll probably be next summer or fall. That's when they start building the Janice Korup Novak Treatment Center. It will be there in honor of you forever."

Chapter 24
I Heard It On the Radio

Joey loved listening to talk radio. Hearing the comments of a cross section of America satisfied his curiosity about the thoughts and dreams of others. In late evening, his AM radio picked up shows from the Midwest, places in Canada and the distant south.

During the day, there were plenty of talk programming choices in Philadelphia. His hometown was one of the nation's talk radio centers, with two 24/7 premier outlets: WIP's endless flow of sports talk and WPHT, which focused on politics and news. But during the five weeks of the Christmas season he took a break and turned to music, listening primarily to FM stations that played round-the-clock Christmas songs.

One night, driving home from a meeting in the Poconos resorts, he was enjoying Melinda's Musical Memories, a syndicated soft-music program interspersed with sappy requests from lovers and all-too cheery call-in regulars. But the music was great, so Joey tuned in despite the callers' silly comments.

It was about 11 p.m. As usual, Melinda was fielding requests from her steady listeners. many of them were newly engaged. But a large number of other callers were happily married couples who were eager to share the secrets of their compatibility and ask for special love tunes.

Occasionally, a lonely listener got through, expressing the blues and requesting a song that a recently deceased or long-gone lover had liked. The age of the callers ranged from teens to grandparents, so it was a good mix of requests, stories and music. One particular on-air conversation affected Joey and caused him to mark the time of the call, so he could follow up on it later.

Alex, from the Midwest was on the phone, talking calmly at first, but soon he began beating around the bush about what he wanted from the DJ goddess. After being pressed several times, the man admitted he had a request that was very unusual and one she probably had never gotten on air before.

Melinda, whose smooth voice contained that rare combination of seductiveness and sappiness, chuckled and told the caller, "This is a family program. Alex. We don't do anything like that over the phone."

Embarrassed, Alex apologized and blurted out he had lost his job eight months earlier. He had been seeking work methodically with no positive results. Apparently, his age of 57 was a drawback.

Melinda, admitting she had never been asked to serve as an employment center, asked Alex the type of job he was seeking and if he would relocate. She took his name off the air and said any listener needing a "computer geek that was very conscientious and willing to work harder than anyone else out there" should call her toll-free line. Her producer would provide Alex's contact information.

Before hanging up, Alex thanked Melinda and, breaking down he began to cry. After regaining his composure, he said, "I can't thank you enough, Melinda. I have a beautiful wife, three wonderful little girls and I love them all very much. But I can't go on being a failure, coming home from my part-time job at the convenience store, knowing I can't give them what they need. They deserve better. I just don't know what I'm going to do."

Apologizing for his inability to maintain his composure, he added, "I just thought, it's Christmastime. Maybe somebody out there will hear this and give me a chance. I guess I'm looking for a Christmas miracle for my family, not just for me, but also for them. They deserve better from me. I don't want my family to think of me as a failure. Thank you, Melinda, and have a Merry Christmas."

Joey had pulled off the road and called the station. He was told he was one of close to a dozen interested businesses that had responded to Alex's plea during the last five minutes. But just as he knew things would work out with Mookie, the little dog on his first day on the job, Joey knew he would be meeting soon with Alex in Henry's office. There they would offer the computer programmer a job and benefits package he wouldn't refuse.

He could hardly wait to arrive home and tell Janice about the wonderful way he had ended his day, helping one deserving person at a time.

CHAPTER 25

'Check Out the Tape'

Joey entered his home in good spirits. Janice had left her husband a note and an unmarked videotape on the kitchen table. "Went to bed. Love you. Take a look at the story on this tape. Here's someone who needs your help."

Joey walked into the living room, turned on the VCR and TV and sat down to watch Janice's recording. An attractive young blonde reporter stood in front of a hospital holding a microphone.

This is WBMD-TV's Mindy Manchester reporting, live—Earlier today, Mark Clemmons, a Dundalk man and single father of three children, said his 14-year-old daughter, Shelley, is in need of a kidney, and he wants to give her his. But the big story on tonight's news is that three years ago Mr. Clemmons had donated one of his kidneys to Shelley. Unfortunately, the father's first donation was rejected by his daughter's body, and his newest request to try again has been turned down. Hospital officials say they won't accept his donation, which would leave him without any kidney. Young Shelley is at the bottom of a very long waiting list. It's important, a Hempstead Hospital spokesperson said, that Shelley receive a transplant in the very near future—or, her situation could prove fatal. Anyone interested in donating a kidney for Shelly should call the WBMD Kidney for Shelley Hotline or go to our web site and click on the picture of Mr. Clemmons and his daughter. This is Mindy Manchester, reporting live at Hempstead Hospital for WBMD-TV NEWS, Baltimore's NUMBER 1 station for all the news you can use!

Joey turned off the set, looked at the clock. It was 1:15 in the morning. He called information, got the Clemmons' home number and dialed the phone.

Joey had no doubt the man would be up and that he would be willing to talk. After a brief conversation, they agreed to meet early the following morning in the hospital coffee shop. Joey knew that after the visit he would be in no condition to drive. He called Father Tom and arranged for the ex-priest to drive him round-trip between Philly and Baltimore.

Hempstead Hospital was in the heart of center city, not too far from the Inner Harbor. Father Tom dropped Joey off at the circle in front of the main door and went to park his car. Joey said he would meet his driver about an hour later in the main lobby.

The hospital's mini eatery was located to the left of the entrance hallway. Joey walked inside and recognized Shelley's father from the TV interview. The troubled man was seated in a booth in the corner. The man's face was tense, displaying a combination of severe concern and intense anger.

Joey walked over, introduced himself and slid onto the dark green leather seat across from Mark Clemmons.

"I don't know why you're here or why I'm here," Mark said, his voice impatient and agitated. He was a rusted spring ready to snap. "I must have been crazy to agree to meet with you. I don't even know what the hell this is about."

Joey looked across at the man with bloodshot eyes and oily, disheveled hair. The man was nervous, tapping his left hand rapidly against the half-filled, white coffee cup.

"I mean, I got doctors to meet, bankers to talk to about getting money for the operation, and that's if we can even find a donor. I mean, I'm sitting up at night praying for a miracle, praying that somebody gets in a fatal accident, nearby, so I can try to haggle for the poor bastard's kidney. I feel like a damn grave robber."

Joey nodded and began to reply.

"Hell, I don't even know who the hell you are!" Mark snapped.

"A friend," Joey said, looking directly into the frustrated man's eyes. And immediately, Joey saw the goodness of the father's soul, by viewing images of his life. In flashes, he saw the man's marriage. Happy parents with three young girls at the beach. A slow-moving funeral procession and graveside ceremony for the man's wife. Shelley and her sisters, along with their father, Mark, hugging in the hospital immediately before the first operation. An argument between Mark and his boss, after the father was told he was in danger of losing his job. The last scene was in Mark Clemmons' bedroom. The man was alone. It was nighttime. There was no light on in the room. A glow from a nearby city streetlamp showed the dark silhouette of a man, kneeling beside his bed, praying the rosary. He was alone, his face intense, his fingers rubbing the worn wooden beads, his lips moving, no sound escaping his lips.

All of the visual information happened in a flash. There was no awkward period of silence. Joey sipped his coffee, then said, "I can help you, but you have to trust me."

"How much do you want?"

"What are you talking about?" Joey said, softly. "I don't . . . ."

"Look. Let's get this out up front. I don't have the kind of money you kind of people want. I'm broke. So you might as well . . . ."

"Who do you think I am?" Joey asked, having a good idea of the reply he would receive.

"A damn black market organ broker," Mark said. "Who the hell else could you be, my long lost guardian angel? You're about the third one I've heard from. The other two wanted around $85,000. That's for the operation and kidney. No guarantees, no questions. They wouldn't take mine and just let me pay for the two operations—Shelley's and mine. Hell, I should have known that. After all, everybody's in business to make a buck. Supply and demand. They got them on ice. One said his is from the Ukraine, the other's is from Cuba. So unless you can settle for less than five grand—which is maybe what I can get when I sell my truck—we're both wasting our time."

Shaking his head, Joey reached across the table and grabbed Mark's wrist.

"What the hell are you doing?" the father began to shout. But his voice trailed off as soon as he noticed a sense of calmness pass through this body. Joey's touch was warm, immediately providing Mark with a feeling of relaxation he had not experienced for weeks. He lifted his head, looked up at Joey and asked, "You can really help?"

Joey nodded and, in a voice that assured the man something good was finally about to happen, said, "I can make her better. I can't explain how, but I can do it. All you have to do is trust me. And I know you will, because you're a good man, a good father, and I'm your last hope."

Mark Clemmons would never remember what Joey looked like or why he believed the stranger's words. Eventually, the entire conversation would cease to exist in the troubled father's memory. However, at that moment he was too exhausted to argue. Desperation and frustration had sapped his ability to think rationally, and nothing other than his daughter's health mattered.

All he knew was that for one moment a complete stranger talked with him in the hospital canteen and then he was at his daughter's bedside, hearing the doctors use the words "an unexplained medical miracle"—and he and Shelley were hugging and crying and thanking God and anyone else within earshot.

Earlier, Father Tom had been waiting in the hospital lobby. He saw Joey talking to the stranger in the booth. The last thing he remembered was his friend reaching across the table and holding onto the other man's wrist, walking with the man into the hallway and taking an elevator going up.

Within what seemed only a minute or two, the priest saw Joey exit slowly from the same elevator and stumble to the floor.

Running to his friend's side, Father Tom lifted Joey and heard him whisper to bring the car around and he would wait on a chair in the lobby. Ten minutes later, the ex-priest dragged Joey's limp body toward the entrance circle and, with the help of a passing attendant, guided his exhausted friend onto the back seat where Joey fell down and slept.

When they reached Joey's house, he was still fatigued and needed Father Tom and Janice to help him up the stairs. After placing him in bed, Janice shut the door and directed Father Tom into the kitchen.

As her confused guest took a seat at the table, Janice poured two cups of coffee. Concerned about Joey's condition, the ex-priest pressed Janice for an explanation.

"He's fine," she said, trying to avoid the topic, but his driver and friend wasn't to be put off.

"Fine? Did you see him? He looks like he should be in intensive care. What's going on?"

"He went down for some tests, that's all," Janice said, avoiding Father Tom's eyes.

"If this was your confession, I'd refuse to give you absolution," he said. "You're not supposed to lie to a priest."

"Ex-priest," she smiled weakly, correcting him.

"Don't try to avoid the issue, Janice," he said, becoming impatient. "Joey has me drive him to Baltimore, *to get some tests done,* and then falls into the car like a dead man. And you tell me he went down for tests? I'm not blind or an idiot. He was talking to some guy in the restaurant, and then he falls out of the elevator like a drunk. Now, something is going on, and you either are going to tell me or you're not. And if you're not, that's fine, but don't lie to me. So, is he critically ill? If so, as his friend, I'd like to know."

Janice raised her head and looked directly into the priest's eyes. "He'll be fine. You'll see. He'll be back at the Inn tomorrow. That's all I can say. If you want to know more, you'll have to ask Joey. That's all I can tell you."

"Fair enough," Father Tom said, and he finished his coffee and left.

* * *

That evening, about midnight, Joey awoke. Janice was reading under a soft light in a chair at the far side of the room.

Turning his head slowly on his pillow, he saw his wife and called her to his side.

"You look horrible," she said, placing the back of her hand against his cheek. "At least you don't have a fever. Are you tired?"

"Exhausted," he said, trying to nod at his wife but unable to lift any part of his body.

"It was all over the Baltimore news tonight," she said. "The father and girl and their doctor. The reporter said everyone is saying it was a miracle. Her kidney is working perfectly. Can you tell me what happened?" she asked.

Still a bit groggy, but in much better condition than he had been in that afternoon, Joey said, "It's fuzzy. I can remember some things, but not everything. I talked to the father in the morning. At first he thought I wanted to sell him a harvested, black market organ. Then, after a while, I grabbed onto his arm, and immediately his attitude changed. It was as if I had unlimited power over him. He believed me and was willing to do whatever I said.

"We went into his daughter's room, There were nurses all around. I could see the girl was scared. Then I stopped time, like Izzy had done to me that first time we met. I knelt by her bed and grabbed her hands. Everything became searing hot. My insides were on fire. My stomach felt like it was holding flames. Then the heat moved toward my shoulders and into my arms and hands. Finally, it passed through my fingers and went into the girl."

Joey paused, took a sip of the water from the glass Janice held to his lips.

After wiping his mouth he continued, "Then, the last thing I remember was seeing a gold or orange-like glow that passed from my hands into her fingers. Her entire hands looked like they were radiating, for only a few seconds, then the brightness disappeared."

Joey said he was so exhausted that he practically had to crawl into the elevator. When he was safely inside he had the sense to have time resume and he was thrilled to see Father Tom waiting in the lobby.

"He might be a problem," Janice said, relating the ex-priest's suspicions and concerns.

"Leave Father Tom to me," Joey said, "and stick to the story. I had a series of complicated tests and I needed a ride home. And you couldn't come because JJ needed you at the house. All right?"

"All right," Janice agreed. Then walking to turn off the light, she said, "You can't do this too often, you know?"

Agreeing, Joey said, "It was brutal. I felt like I was dying. My insides were twisted, searing, and the pain was terrible. But, when I saw that glow, whatever it was, pass from me into that girl, I knew she was going to be better, going to live. And to know that I was the instrument, the tool that God used to help her and her family, that made it worth all the pain. But," he added after a brief pause, "it's impossible to do this again soon. I just can't, even if I want to. It's just too much. You know what I mean?"

"Joey, I saw your nearly dead body when you came home ten hours ago. I understand. Now, get some more sleep. You're going to have to deal with Father Tom and give him a story he can believe. And he's not a fool. After all, the man's made a career of listening to professional liars every Saturday in the confessional."

Chapter 26

Homeless and Cold

The two men of the family, Joey and JJ, were out on the town, shopping in Center City a week before Christmas. Of course, the old Wanamaker's store was one of their first stops. Even though the department store had been bought out by a competitor years ago, its annual Christmas light show was a favorite Philadelphia tradition that the new buyers had continued.

Joey still marveled at the beautiful holiday program. He particularly enjoyed seeing JJ's eyes fill with delight as the young boy responded to the music and dancing lights featuring snowmen, Santa, reindeer, stars and sparkling snowflakes.

After consuming cheese steaks and fries at a corner deli, the two carefree shoppers continued their merry seasonal march through the cold winds of downtown.

As they turned a corner beside a high-rise office building, the burst of cold, steel-canyon wind slammed against the walkers. Men were knocked off balance, and youngsters held onto their elders' coat-tails and legs.

Seated on a heat vent, about 50 feet from the intersection were several homeless men. Multiple layers of ragged clothing wrapped around their limbs made their bodies seem like tattered, inflatable broken dolls.

Pulling on his father's hand, JJ stopped, put down his packages and pointed to the gray-haired, older man holding an open cigar box. He was rattling a few coins to attract the attention and sympathy of passers-by.

Using his hands and speaking simultaneously, JJ said, "I want to give him some money, for food, for Christmas."

A year before, Joey would have told his son "No way!" He would have said that the man was probably lazy, didn't want to work, and that there always was a job for someone who tried hard enough to find it. Joey would have commanded his son to "Spend your money on someone who would appreciate it, who deserves it."

But now Joey, the Keeper, knew better. *Who deserved it more than the poor and those without hope?* Joey smiled and told JJ he could do what he wanted. It was his money. The boy pulled out two dollars and began to walk toward the beggar.

Grabbing his son's free hand, Joey walked beside him. But before JJ's hand dropped the bills into the Phillies cigar box, the Keeper of the Coins stopped time—for everyone except himself and the gray-haired stranger.

"He's a nice looking boy," the man said to Joey.

Looking down on the dirty creature with his stained clothes, mis-matched shoes and straggly hair, Joey replied, "He takes after his mother. She's kind and caring, too."

"I also was, once," the beggar said, "But that was before I . . . ."

"Gave up hope, lost your faith," Joey said, "after your family died in the fire."

"Yeah. The fire," the beggar replied, his eyes remembering a far-away scene from long ago, but not long enough to be erased from his memory. "I was at the office, working late—again," the man said.

"Your name is Martin. Martin Blake," Joey said, as he and the stranger conversed amid human statues scattered across the silent frigid city scene.

"That's me. Financial analyst, MBA degree. Had to stay late at work, chose to ignore something that was telling me to get home, that I was going to be needed. Had to . . ."

Joey finished Martin's memory, "Had to wait for the opening stock market quotes from Tokyo, Munich and then London. Your boss needed the information the next morning. If you didn't have the report done, you could kiss away the promotion, get bumped off the fast track."

"But I would still have a family," Martin said, beginning to sob, "if I had gone home on time. It was important. It was my wife's birth-day. We had reservations for dinner. Belinda, our daughter was at the neighbor's overnight. We were supposed to go out, be together."

"She called you a half dozen times," Joey said, "but you never picked up the phone. You didn't want to tell her how late you would be, didn't want to disappoint her, get into an argument. You knew that you didn't have a good excuse, so instead you ignored her."

Martin began to cry, explaining that he put aside the calls from his wife, but he couldn't do that to his boss. No way he could mess up the wonderful opportunity, the big chance to move up a few rungs on the ladder of financial success. And when he finally arrived home his house was nearly gone. He got there in time to see his young daughter screaming, comforted in the neighbors' arms, as medical examiners carried a dark green plastic bag out of his home. The sack contained his wife's charred body.

"They said she had gotten drunk. The investigators reported she must have lit a few logs in the fireplace and passed out. They found her lying near the fireplace, burned. She never woke up."

Martin looked up at Joey. "It was my fault. She never drank, wasn't used to the hard stuff, couldn't handle it. Two glasses of wine and she was knocked out. She got drunk to spite me. I guess she thought I would find her when I got home and have to carry her to bed. Her way of showing me she was upset. So instead of celebrating on her birthday, she died on her birthday. Strange, or maybe poetic justice. What do you think, Keeper?"

Joey didn't talk, didn't reply. He just listened.

"I should have been there," Martin added. "I should have been home. But it was that damned report. I would make more money, be able to acquire more possessions, a nicer car, that dream beach house we had always talked about."

Laughing, Martin opened his arms, indicating for Joey to look at the four bags the beggar carried on his body throughout the day and night. "How much stuff do I need? Tell me. Everything I have is in these plastic bags. Everything I lost is seared into my memory and my heart. And for what? For what, Keeper? Tell me."

Joey didn't have an answer. Apparently, some things even he didn't have the power to fix, couldn't make right.

"I haven't seen my daughter in eight years," Martin moaned. "She's gone, far off, to live with strangers. So," Martin said, pulling a half-filled bottle from beneath one of his tattered sacks, "I get through each hour, each day, with the help of this." He tossed back his head and swallowed a long dram of brown liquid. "Ahhhh! That's my medicine, Keeper. It's my curse and my cure.

"So, tell me, friend, can you help me? Can you take back any of the damn pain, help me relive my life, give me another chance? Or are you just another do-gooder, out to put a coat of salve on your guilt by throwing a few dollars my way, to convince yourself you care about the poor?"

Joey knelt down, shook his head, and said, "I can't help cure your soul, Martin. Your burden's too heavy. Only God and you can work that out. All I can do is tell you I understand you're hurting. I also know I can't even try to imagine the intensity of your regret. I wish I could do more, but then . . . ."

"Then what good are you, Keeper? If you can't do anything for me," the beggar snapped, "then go to hell, and take your damn son and his two dollars away with you. I'll need a lot more than that to buy enough liquor store medicine to erase my nightmares."

Joey stood up and restarted time. He held onto JJ as the boy dropped the pair of ones into Martin's box. The troubled man gazed ahead, as if he was unaware of the youngster's kind gesture. Then Joey shoved a fifty dollar bill into Martin's hand.

The beggar grasped Joey's fingers and held onto them for several seconds. "Good-bye Keeper. Remember, you can't save the whole world. That was never part of the deal."

Joey yanked his hand from Martin's grasp and pulled JJ closer as they hurried down the street. And in his mind he saw a vision of the troubled beggar, sometime in the near future, passed out on a landing of the Broad Street Subway. There were three empty bottles of cheap liquor at his side. Two police officers were standing above the body, careful to stand back from the pungent smell as they waited for the coroner to arrive and shove Martin's lifeless shell in a green plastic bag.

But perhaps, Joey thought, *that was to be Martin's way of escaping his past. Then he would finally be able to meet his wife and tell her he was sorry.*

CHAPTER 27

Father Tom's Story

Joey was on the cordless phone, pacing back and forth behind the Welcome Inn bar. Henry was on the other end of the call, pleading for some time off. Christmas was only a few days away.

"Joey, it's Christmas week. We cannot keep up with your schedule. You simply must slow down. I have to allow my people some holiday time off. And I suggest that you, as well, take some time to rest. Spend an extended period of relaxation with your family. By giving them additional attention, you will help both me and my staff."

"I thought you liked having something worthwhile to do, Henry?" Joey said, smiling at the remark. A part of him enjoyed aggravating the usually poised and stiff-laced legal professional.

"Enough, Joey. Please. I am suggesting just a few days' respite. So the ladies here may be able to shop and bake some Christmas cookies." Henry lowered his voice and whispered through the phone, trying to convey the urgency of his request. "I am afraid I may have some staffing issues—like major resignations—if they don't receive some relief."

Joey agreed to Henry's request and promised to slow down. He said he would only call the accountant if there was a major problem.

Not satisfied with that answer, Henry replied, "I am not a fool, Joey, you and you alone can make sure there is no major problem. Don't you understand? You spend all your time going out and looking for trouble. It doesn't usually come *to you*. You go out and drag it in, from out of the bowels of wherever it has been happily hiding, for *us* to deal with. So, please, stay put for a few days. Do you understand?"

"Fine." he replied. "I'll lay low until after New Year's. But then you better be ready to step up the pace."

A soft and quite unprofessional groan at the other end of the line was followed by a quick thank you and short click.

Joey smiled, knowing Henry was smart enough to put an end to their conversation before the Keeper thought of something else that he needed accomplished. But while he had every intention of avoiding Henry for the next 10 days, emergency circumstances were about to arise that were beyond the Keeper's control.

* * *

By 10:30 in the morning, the Inn began to fill as the first lunch crowd regulars started to arrive. Plus, business usually picked up the week before Christmas and continued through New Year's Day. People stocked up on booze to give away as gifts. Others came in for a few hours while they were back home, visiting relatives. They all came in to catch up with longtime friends and talk over old times, see who had died, was divorced or in jail.

Buddha, a new face that had appeared in the Inn during the last month, was among the late morning crowd. A night shift worker, he arrived at the same time, several days each week. The stranger had a pleasant demeanor and seemed to be working his way into a regulars' slot, but time would tell. Like a lot of newcomers and sometimers, Buddha could disappear as quickly as he had materialized. Since Joey had not heard from Izzy in some time, the bartending Keeper looked upon any new arrival as a potential visit from an Izzy-in-disguise.

The short, round-shaped character with a short black beard and distinctive Oriental nickname didn't go unnoticed. Above his belt line, Buddha's stomach protruded straight out, giving the impression he was carrying twins. Whenever Buddha headed for the men's room he caused snickers and comments throughout the bar, as the tip of his ample, extended stomach would hit the swinging door before his arms, making it seem to open magically.

Unable to squeeze into a booth, Buddha usually set up shop at a table near the poolroom. As someone with an opinion on any subject, Buddha happily discussed anything with anyone who paused near his bar room throne. On this particular morning, the topic was whether to place garland and lights on the *Rocky* statue, which stood near the bottom of the Art Museum steps. Everyone in Philly knew the well-known artwork was a dangerous topic and the source of strong feelings among long time locals—many of whom regarded the popular tourist attraction as Philly's answer to Rome's Michelangelo sculpture of *David*.

"I tell you guys," Buddha said, "it's not art, and it shouldn't be anywhere near the museum. I say they should put a cable around the stupid thing's neck, lift it up with a crane and toss it in the Delaware River. It doesn't even deserve a strand of tinsel. About the only thing that I would do is shove the bottom end of a candy cane up Rocky's big fat, broken nose!"

"You gotta problem with the Rock, Buddha?" Jersey Jack asked, his speech slurred from a long morning of non-stop elbow tilting.

"Yeah," Buddha, replied. "Your so-called Philly hero doesn't even own a house in the city, and he only comes back every four or five years to do a new movie about an outta-shape, punch-drunk has been. But the best part is that the nitwits in South Philly think Rocky is a *real* person. And when you tell the morons the truth, they get pissed off. It's as if I told 'em that God doesn't live in Heaven and that Hell doesn't exist, which, I add, is true."

"Hell there ain't no Hell!" Jack snapped. "I been there and back lots of times. Had dreams about bein' stuck in Hell. My old job was Hell. Where the Hell ya think they got the term 'hot as Hell,' Buddha?"

A few of the other customers offered Jack some weak scattered applause and encouraging shouts. Realizing the crowd had his back, the Rocky fan smiled and continued his defense, "And as for the Rock, I know he's real. Plus I know a guy that works with Pauly at the slaughter house, over on Delaware Ave., where the Rock pounded on that frozen meat before his fights. So if Pauly is real, then the Rock hasta be real. Besides, why the hell would they spend all that money on a statue and put it up if the guy ain't real? You're fulla crap, Buddha, and I hate like hell to use that kinda damn talk around Christmastime."

Struggling to stand and extend his arms into the air, Buddha spun his frame around the room like a slow-moving top, shouting, "Are you people hearing this? Do you believe your freakin' ears? This is exactly what I've been talking about. Jack and the rest of you illiterates think the *Rocky* statue is art and that the character is REAL! He is *make believe*, people. He's a freakin' South Philly fairy tale that's flying out of control."

Boos and abusive shouts, accompanied by rolled-up napkins and broken pretzel pieces, soared across the room in Buddha's direction.

"Ain't no fairies in South Philly, you fat dipshit!" someone yelled from the rear of the poolroom.

Before things got out of control, Joey shouted at the guys to pick up the trash and calm down. He ordered Buddha to put a lid on the *Rocky* conversation or take a hike until things cooled off.

After mumbling complaints about restricting his right of free speech, Buddha gathered both flaps of his coat. Unable to fasten the buttons, he tried to pull the material around his ample girth. While the disgruntled patron stomped toward the exit, several pool players began singing the *Rocky* theme. "Da Da—Da Da Da—Da Da—Da Da Da," they shouted in out-of-tune laughter, causing Buddha to turn around and shoot his opponents a matching pair of obscene farewell gestures. When the door slammed behind the rotund regular in training, the merry crowd applauded itself and a quieter atmosphere slowly settled throughout the building.

Uncle Lou arrived about a half-hour before noon to help with the midday rush. Joey appreciated the assistance. By 1:30 p.m., things had slowed down to a manageable level. As Uncle Lou was getting ready to take a deposit to the bank, he pulled Joey aside and whispered, "Did you check out Father Tom? He's gotta heavy load on and it's still early. How long's he been here?"

Joey hadn't noticed when the ex-priest had arrived. "A few hours, I guess. Came in during lunch, when the place was a zoo."

"Well, slow the padre down or he's gonna be passed out in his confessional before we say grace for dinner. I'm tellin' ya, he's goin' hot and heavy. What's his damn problem?"

Joey shrugged. "Don't know, but I'll be sure to find out."

Shortly after Uncle Lou left, Joey signaled Long John to take over the bar. With two cups of coffee in hand, Joey settled in across the table in Father Tom's booth and shoved a steaming mug toward the priest.

"How about a warm one, Tom?"

Two heavy eyelids lifted and stared at the gift bearer. "How about another *cold* one instead, Joey?"

"Later, Tom. You need to slow down," Joey advised. "It's still early. You have to stay in shape for your appointments. You'll probably have a steady line of free advice seekers heading your way in the next hour or two. Gotta have a clear head, be sharp."

Frowning, Tom replied, "That's me. Mister Advice. The Holy Answer Man. Or how about The Defrocked, Has Been Priest?"

Silence ruled the booth for about 20 seconds. When the quiet became uncomfortable, Joey asked, "You still upset with me about our trip to Baltimore?"

The ex-priest laughed and took another swallow of his beer. "You kidding? You don't have to tell me anymore than the lies you and your wife already gave me about that strange ride. That's your business, but don't think I'm totally ignorant. Something strange happened that day. But, that's none of my affair. Besides," he looked away from Joey's stare. "I've got my own problems to deal with."

Thinking he had just been offered an invitation to talk, Joey asked, "You wanna talk about it, Tom? Kick it around, whatever it is?"

"For what purpose, Joey? Other than to stir up bad memories, there's not much reason is there? I mean, what are they going to do, give me back my church? Let me back in the club?"

"I don't understand, Tom. Come on, talk to me, get it off your chest."

Smiling, the priest stared across the table. A few silent moments passed, time for him to consider Joey's offer. Nodding toward the bar lined with colorful bottles containing brown, tan and clear hard whiskey, the ex-priest said, "Get me a little *real* lubricant, Joey, and I'll give you the whole sordid story. That's the cost of my sad tale."

By the time Joey returned with two shot glasses and a bottle of Seagram's 7, Tom seemed ready to open up. People in the bar business noticed how people got sentimental during the holidays, especially the poor souls who lived alone. Father Tom, Joey thought, apparently was no exception.

After taking a strong swallow of a shot and downing a chaser of fresh beer, Tom began his story. He provided Joey with a bit of background about his clerical career, then offered details about the events—seven years earlier—that ended his active religious life.

Tom had been ordained a priest in a lesser-known rite of the Roman Catholic Church. It was a national organization with more than a hundred thousand members, and it observed most of the major sacraments and beliefs of the main Catholic church. However, disgruntled members had split off from Rome and formed their own rite about 50 years earlier, because its followers and clergy wanted to maintain many of the older, long-established and familiar Catholic traditions, hymns and prayers.

Father Tom was working at St. Romonius' National Church near Paoli, a fast-growing and affluent area located about 18 miles west of Philadelphia. Tom's boss and the small church's rector—which was the equivalent of what most people refer to as a pastor—was a moody, ultra old-fashioned cleric.

"This guy," Tom said, "he was a real pain in the ass. He was no Barry Fitzgerald from *Going My Way,* Joey. He was big, grouchy and downright mean. He wouldn't say two words to you, unless he wanted to find fault. And he spent his evenings writing up complaints about me—and anyone else who was assigned to his place—and mailed them into the assistant bishop—*his cousin.*"

"You're kidding!"

Tom shook his head, and then added, "The place should have installed a revolving door on the rectory. No assistant lasted more than a year. The guys sentenced there before me did anything they could to get transferred out of the place. It was a living hell.

"Anyway, I was there about nine months. Spent most of my time—including eating my meals at a local diner—as far away as possible from Monsignor Miserable. That's the name I gave him."

Pausing, Tom took a breath, and seemed to be looking off in the distance, apparently dredging up a long buried memory he had wanted to forget. "Then," he said, "there was the *incident*."

"What do you mean, *incident*?"

"For me it turned out to be a life-changing event. It had to do with a problem involving some altar boys. Were you an altar boy, Joey?"

The bartender nodded.

"Good," Tom said, "so you know what it was like. A bunch of kids, in the prime years of high jinx, combined with raging hormones and serious social pressures, and tossed into a complex position. It demanded they be little angels for the length of the Mass and then they would break loose, raise hell and goof off. Just like all kids their age."

"That's a good picture of the situation," Joey said, smiling as he recalled the antics and games he and his fellow Knights of the Altar would play in the hidden passageways and basement of the church.

Tom stressed that his esteemed rector liked his wine. After years of having a healthy nip early each morning, many long-time priests looked forward to kicking off their day by unlocking the church's wine cabinet. Unfortunately, two of the older altar boys had arrived early, picked the lock on the liquor cabinet, consumed about 95 percent of the holy wine and refilled the glass cruets with tap water.

"When my rector got to the part in the Mass that he liked best," Tom said, "where he took his customary belt of holy grape juice, his palate was shocked and left unsatisfied. Enraged, he simmered through the remainder of the Mass, which he completed at lightening speed. Afterward, he stormed into the sacristy and let the anger, which he had been holding in during the service, explode. He began shouting at the two boys. Unfortunately for them, one thought it was funny and began to laugh. That enraged the rector, who punched the boy in the face.

"When the blood began gushing out of his nose, the kid tried to run out of the church, but the rector completely lost control. He tackled the boy and began beating him mercilessly.

"About that time, I walked into the sacristy, to get ready for my Mass," Father Tom recalled. "There was blood all over the floor. I mean, he really must have smashed the poor kid with a good one. One boy was kneeling in a corner hiding. The other kid was lying on his chest, with his arms spread out, crucifixion style, mumbling something to himself. He was naked from the waist up, and the rector was over by the sink, trying to wash the blood out of the kid's shirt.

"I demanded to know what was going on, and the rector turned to me—with his eyes bulging out of his sockets—and said, 'They have committed a sacrilege and are destined for hell, unless they repent.'

"I told the boys to get up and go home, but *my boss* started shouting that they had consumed the blood of Christ. That the Lord was within their sin-infested bodies and they had to be cleansed. They would remain, he said, until he decided they had been made pure and punished for the theft of the holy sacramentals."

Father Tom paused to toss down another shot and take a sip of his fast-disappearing beer. Joey waited for more.

"Like a very bad movie, huh?" Tom asked. "I guess you want me to go on to the climax?"

"Yeah," Joey said, nodding. "But I don't think it turns out with justice being served."

"Very observant," Father Tom said, "but that's not too hard to figure out. After all, I'm here, crying the blues to you, and Monsignor Miserable is in charge of training new recruits. And his cousin is a bigshot at our Northeaster Province headquarters, in a fancy mansion right here in Philadelphia. Pretty scary, wouldn't you say?"

"Sure would," Joey agreed. "So tell me how he got out of it and why you got busted."

Father Tom smiled, "One word, five letters. Starts with an M."

"Money," Joey said.

"Correct, my friend. Wealth can be the source of either trouble or ecstasy, good or ill. It depends upon who controls it. Far too often, it is at the disposal of those who are weak, or who eventually are corrupted by its seductive power. You see, Joey, no matter who you are, if you have a lot of money and power, it eventually will ruin you. As it did my rector, Prelate Roman Branko, and his very close relation, Auxiliary Bishop Antek Branko."

Father Tom continued, "Roman was raving like a madman. I tried to reason with him, get him to let the boys go, but he went nuts. He was cursing, throwing things around. When I couldn't convince him to drop the whole thing, and I was afraid that someone was going to be seriously hurt, I ran back to the rectory and called the police.

"By the time they got there, about 30 minutes later, the boys were gone, the place was immaculate. And the cops looked at me like I was insane. Roman must have had the housekeeper working in overdrive to clean up the blood in the church. He denied there was any altercation and said I had been a very serious problem in the parish, as a result of my *alcoholic tendencies*.

He instructed the police to talk to the bishop's representative, a slick-talking weasel named Heckbert, who must have broken the sound barrier getting to our church so quickly. Of course, he verified the rector's version that nothing out of sorts had occurred. Apparently, Roman had come to his senses and called his cousin, Antek, who told him to clam up and let the province representative handle everything."

"Didn't the cops believe anything you said?"

"Joey, can you imagine what happens when two lifer, Irish cops talk to a bigshot representative from the local bishop's office, wearing a $400 suit and leaning against a black Mercedes? He pulls them aside, and *confidentially* tells them about the parish's *problem priest*, namely me, who the rector has been having a horrible time with. Who do you think they're going to believe? "

"What about the kids? Didn't they back up your version?"

Laughing, Tom slammed his beer bottle flat against the table. "Do you know what it costs to go to a private Catholic high school and then college? That's at least eight years of high-priced tuition. Well, whatever it was, it was a lot. Those two kids were getting set up for life while the cops were getting schmoozed by the church's official spin master. The boys were given a free ride, all tuition, books, room and board at St. Martin's Prep School and College, out on the Main Line. Do you think their parents were going to have them say anything other than agree with rector Roman and his well-connected cousin, who sat at the right hand of the bishop of the province? They were all on the same page, reading a two-word script—'Nothing happened.' "

"So you got screwed?"

"Bingo! No complaints. No witnesses. No problem. Except for me. You want to know if I got shafted? That's putting it rather simply," Father Tom said. "After a rather intimidating meeting with the province attorney and three sessions with the province psychologist, I was designated 'unbalanced' and 'delusional,' as well as a 'disruptive influence.' So I got a new assignment—sent on a one-way trip to a retreat house near Niagara Falls. It's a hideaway place where many of the provinces on the East Coast—from your Latin rite and the lesser known Catholic orders—send rebellious and uncooperative clergy.

"On my floor, there were six pedophiles, about eight alcoholics and three guys who couldn't keep their hands off their housekeepers and the school nuns. Oh, and one guy who claimed he was really Jesus Christ and wanted us to be his 18 or so disciples for the Second Coming." Laughing at the memory, Tom added, "He was rather convincing at times, and at least the most entertaining of our troupe of misfits."

"How long did you stay?"

"Slightly over two weeks. I had been assigned there for four months, but I couldn't take it, so I left. Came back here, to Philly, and sent out letters and resumes trying to get a parish priest job anywhere in the country. But they had put me in long term limbo."

"Limbo?" Joey replied, recalling the term's theological definition. "Like where the dead babies that didn't live long enough to be baptized used to go?"

"Right. Our sect still has Limbo on the books. But your gang is getting rid of it, along with Purgatory and, eventually, I won't be surprised when your Latin rite declares the Devil, himself, is no more and never was. But that's another set of issues and not part of my story."

The priest regrouped, explaining every province, church society or order of priests, nuns or monks has a troublemaker file. It's a list of religious considered hard for authorities to deal with. When a name is placed on that list, it's circulated throughout the country and abroad.

"After your name is entered," Tom said, "it's impossible to obtain a position—whether clerical, administrative or janitorial—in our sect or with any other Catholic-related institution."

"You were blackballed," Joey said.

"Correct. Placed in religious unemployment hell and destined to remain there until someone in authority set me free—and that turned out to be never. I got one single offer, from an Indian reservation in God-Knows-Where, New Mexico. It sounded like a real hellhole, but I was going to take it. I even agreed to pay my own way out there. The night before I was going to leave on a very long bus ride, I got a last minute call telling me they *couldn't hire* me. That was it. No further explanation. No nothing. Not even an 'I'm sorry.' I was like the Black Death in the Middle Ages, any contact with me and your career was over. I was as welcome as a hooker walking the streets with a 'Free AIDS' sign hanging from her neck."

Conversation stopped for a few moments as the priest took a sip of his drink and avoided eye contact with Joey or anyone else in the room. Joey didn't try to break the silence. Any comment would have seemed meaningless and contribute nothing to the situation.

Father Tom pushed away the awkward silence, explaining that at least he still has his psychology degree. "So here I am, working for the state, in a filthy nut farm, trying to counsel anyone they give me. And never being able to go back and do what I dreamed of doing since I was a little kid, saying Mass and serving as a messenger for the Lord."

"Is there any higher authority to talk to, to get you reinstated?"

Stifling his urge to scream, Tom glared at Joey and said, "Did you hear anything I said, Joey? This is big business. All these guys are hooked up. Unless you've got a direct line to the Pope or ten grand for a bribe, they give you that pious look, the knowing smile, a kindly nod, and then they have one of their lackeys tell you someone *will be in touch.* That's their way of saying, 'You screwed up big time, so hit the road.'

" You see, Joey, I've got dirt, know things that I shouldn't. I'm a liability. If they ever let me back in, they'd always have to watch over their shoulders. They'd be afraid one day I'd threaten to use what I know against them. The easiest way to solve the problem is to cut me loose and keep me at a distance."

Shaking his head, Tom added, "I can't tell you how many letters I've written to province headquarters. I think I received one reply. The rest, I imagine, just disappear. Never get to the archbishop or his staff. But I'm not surprised. Antek Branko is in a perfect position to intercept anything I try. And who would believe me anyway? Come on, you just heard the story. Doesn't the whole thing sound nuts to you?"

Joey didn't reply. He was also concerned these were supposed to be holy, caring people. But they had ruined a good man's life.

Reading Joey's mind, Tom said, "Yeah, Joey. You think all priests are wonderful because they wear a black collar with that little white box in the front of their neck. That you should be able to trust them with your kids, your family, ask them for guidance about your most personal problems. Well, my naïve friend, take this from someone who's been a member of the club, there are good ones and there are bad ones, just like in every big company.

"Religious people have no corner on the goodness market. And, unfortunately, the higher some of them climb, the worse a few of them become. Just like in the outside world. That's because it's just another big business spinning out of control and run by big wheels, whose egos need to be fed. They think they're the smartest people in the room. They sit in throne-like chairs, and they tell you they're the only ones who are able to see the *big picture*—that all of us peasants are too uneducated to comprehend. But these so-called holy ones have total control over other people's lives, careers and souls.

"The sad thing is, some of them spend more time protecting their positions than caring for the people who have next to nothing. All that talk about loving thy neighbor is for show, Joey. You won't find any saints among the bigshots in plush offices wearing tailored cassocks. They're religious CEOs that don't forgive and forget—but they're quick to cover up for their own kind. The real saints are dishing out watered-down soup in ghetto homeless shelters. You never see the workers in the projects racing to flash big smiles in front of the TV cameras. They're too busy doing good."

Both men remained silent for a few seconds, then Father Tom looked up and said, "I think it's amazing that the master cover-up guy, Antek, is second in command here in Philly. And you know where they put the nut I worked for, the sick bastard who beat up the kid?"

Joey waited for the answer.

"He's in charge of a seminary in Maryland. Imagine that? He beat the hell out of these kids, and they send him away to be in charge of the training of more of them. Imagine what the atmosphere of that place must be like, with him at the top, molding young minds."

Nodding, Joey knew his face displayed disappointment.

Then, downing the last remnant from the long neck bottle, Father Tom said, "You know what the worst part for me is, Joey? Want to hear the end of my sad saloon confession?"

The bartender nodded.

"Being a priest without a church on Christmas Eve. That, my patient listener, was my greatest joy and now my biggest struggle. Up on the altar, a full church, flickering candles being held in procession, beautiful decorations and the choir singing those wonderful ageless songs. And on that night everyone sang along, unembarrassed, boldly, reliving their youth and family traditions with each familiar carol and hymn. That is what I have missed for the last seven years. The joy of being a part of the magic of the Christmas miracle. That's what rips at my heart the most."

"So you don't go to church, at all?"

"Never," Father Tom admitted, his eyes starting to fill up with tears. "If I go into a church at any time of the year, even just to kneel and pray, my stomach feels like it's being torn apart. If I dared to go in at Christmas, I would lose it. So I have my own quiet Christmas celebration, at home."

Joey looked, waiting for an explanation.

"I know this sounds insane. It might even prove they were right about me after all, that I should have been put away. I say Mass in my apartment, on my kitchen table. I do it every morning, Joey. I'll do it at midnight on Christmas Eve again this year. Isn't that nuts?"

Reaching across and grabbing Tom by the forearm, Joey replied, "No Father Tom, not nuts at all. After all, you're a priest, a very good person."

Offering a weak wave of thanks, he said, "I guess you're sorry you opened up that can of worms, huh, Joey?"

"Not really, Father. It helps me understand a lot. Maybe this Christmas will be easier to handle, just knowing someone who cares realizes how hard it is for you. But no matter, you'll still be at our place for Christmas dinner, right?"

Smiling, the ex-priest said, "If you still want me, I'd be thrilled to come."

"We won't start without you, Father. And you'll say grace."

"Thanks," the priest said, weakly. "I'm looking forward to it. After all, where else do I have to go?"

Joey stood up, patted his friend on the shoulder and headed to the old phone booth at the rear of the bar. He had to make a call and break a promise. Joey needed to get Henry and his staff back on the job, right away.

Chapter 28

Henry in High Gear

When Henry saw the caller ID on his private cell phone, his body cringed. Cursing, he knew Joey wouldn't let up, wouldn't give Henry and his staff a break. Summoning his assistant into his office, Henry directed her to answer his phone and tell the caller that her boss was out for the rest of the year.

Listening from across the room, Henry rolled his eyes as the experienced worker got nowhere with her excuses. Joey demanded that she put Henry on the phone, and, if he refused to answer, she should tell her boss Joey was going to close his account.

Annoyed that he had tossed his employee into the no-win situation, Henry ran to her side, grabbed the phone and snapped, quite uncharacteristically, "Joey, you promised, damnit! Just three hours ago you gave me your word that I would not hear from you until next year! Can't you allow me any time to myself? You are out of control, Joey. I am warning you, you are pushing me too far!"

After waiting a respectable amount of time for Henry to exhaust his diatribe of complaints, Joey dictated a list of what he needed accomplished by the following morning.

"I want a private meeting with Antek Branko, the first auxiliary bishop of the Northeastern Province of the TeDeus Slavic Rite Church, by tomorrow afternoon or Wednesday morning at the latest. I think their headquarters is located just off Broad Street, not too far from your office."

Henry exploded again. "Joey! Are you in your right mind? Do I have to remind your that this is Christmas week? Wednesday is Christmas Eve. This is their big day. It's like New Year's Eve for Dick Clark. No assistant bishop is going to see you until after New Year's at the earliest—if I can even manage to schedule an audience for you then."

"Are you done?" Joey said, calmly.

"You have more?" Henry snapped. "You are telling me you want *more* than this from me?"

Joey added another shocker. "I also want Roman Branko, rector of Saint Brendan the Navigator's Seminary, in on the meeting." Before Henry replied with another outburst, Joey added, "He's the Philly bigshot's cousin. The seminary is somewhere outside Annapolis. But I'll be reasonable and allow him to be present on a video conference call, if he can't come up here in person. But" Joey added, "I'll bet you any amount that he will be there and wearing a set of Jingle Bells."

"Well, well," Henry sang sarcastically, adding, "how wonderfully considerate of you, Mister Novak. You want me to arrange a meeting with two of the most respected members of the clergy, both of whom are very busy, with only one day's notice. In addition, you want this minor miracle accomplished only two days before Christmas." Breathing out heavily, Henry asked, "And why, Joey, should these gentlemen agree to meet with you?"

"I only need about 20 minutes," Joey said.

"Wonderful, however, I repeat, *why* should they agree?"

"You tell them that the CEO of the Melchior Charitable Trust wants to discuss a seven-figure contribution to each province as a special Christmas present. I guarantee you, they both will squeeze me into their busy schedules."

Henry was silent a moment, and then added, "I guess you will tell me eventually what this is about?"

"Keep your pen handy," Joey said, "because before I walk in there, with YOU, we're going to need a number of documents that I am sure you can get, even though, I'll admit, it's short notice. And I know I will owe you big time for this one."

Resigned to the situation, Henry said, "All right. Let us begin. I have a feeling I'm going to need to demand that some of the staff work overtime."

"Pay them triple time and add in a bonus if you have to, then put it on my bill," Joey said.

"Do not worry, Joey," Henry said firmly, "you are going to pay a high price for this last minute caper."

Smiling from his phone booth hideaway in the Inn, the Keeper gave Henry a detailed rundown of the situation—including names, dates and the documentation he thought they would need. Joey was confident his experienced attorney/accountant would supplement the suggestions with whatever was necessary to accomplish their goal. Henry's only reply was an impersonal dial tone, indicating their conversation was over.

When he hung up, Joey knew what Father Tom said was correct: *Wealth can be associated with good or ill, depending upon whom has control of it. Too often, it is at the disposal of those who are evil or who have been corrupted by its seductive power.*

Once again, Joey knew, he was going to make sure his power and money were used to do the right thing.

CHAPTER 29
The Showdown

Henry and Joey were seated in an impressively paneled library that oozed wealth and Old World craftsmanship and had witnessed many sessions of intense negotiations. It was early, 8:50 a.m. on Christmas Eve morning. Amazingly, both clerics had agreed to meet, in person, with Mr. Joseph Novak and Mr. Henry Staltzmann, representatives of the Melchior Charitable Trust.

The previous day, Henry had faxed details about the foundation's portfolio to the province's treasurer, providing information on Melchior's attention-grabbing assets, highlighting its recent generous charitable distributions. Obviously impressed with what they saw, the two high ranking religious administrators were quick to respond to the millions of dollars that had been dangled as bait to attract their personal attention.

Precisely at 9 a.m., a skinny clerical drone, who was well dressed in a delicately embroidered black cassock, led the visitors into the Northeastern Province auxiliary bishop's office. With a slight bow, Joey and Henry's mute guide stopped and pointed a limp hand toward the thick carved door that was the gateway into the inner chamber.

As the visitors entered the palatial suite, which could have served as a setting for the throne room in King Arthur's castle, the two men were slightly shocked at the stark contrasts between the two clerical cousins.

One was large, the other small; one string-bean skinny, one pumpkin-round obese; one's voice was thin and shrill, the other's fat and bellowing. It was Stan and Ollie—Laurel and Hardy—in religious disguise. The thin man, Antek, was second in command of the religious syndicate headquartered in Philly. His fat cousin, Roman, was in charge of the seminary, to which he had been exiled in rural Maryland, a few months after the child beating incident. *One was overseer of the Delaware River province*, thought Joey, *while the other was hidden away out of sight, near the top of the Chesapeake Bay.*

"Welcome, welcome," Antek/Stan, the Philadelphia host, chirped out in greeting.

Roman/Ollie was silent, resembling a large dark pear. He made no attempt to—or perhaps was unable to—rise from his overstuffed chair.

As introductions were exchanged, Joey stared at Roman Branko, the beefy seminary administrator who would be the main target during the upcoming exchange. The man's round, pious face was a stretched grinning mask, hiding the control-freak cleric who rarely revealed his true self to the public.

"So, gentlemen," host Antek Branko said, "we are pleased to meet you both, and we are curious as to what precisely my cousin and I can do for you? How, gentlemen, can we be of spiritual assistance?"

Joey and Henry took their seats in padded wine-red chairs, trimmed in ornately carved dark wood. The four men were seated around a moderate-sized table and, as he began the conversation, Henry carefully displayed more than a half-dozen leather-bound folders on the highly polished surface.

"We are here, Your Excellencies," Henry said with a slight nod of respect, "on behalf of the Melchior Charitable Trust, an organization dedicated to the perpetuation of goodwill and the protection of the weak and oppressed throughout the world."

"Commendable. Highly commendable," Roman Branko's fat lips mumbled, his comment sounding more like a growl. As the man's paw lifted a cup of coffee toward his lips, the delicate imported china resembled a small child's toy teacup.

Joey and Henry smiled at the acknowledgment.

Interjecting a comment that he was sure would demonstrate his religious knowledge, the Philadelphia host proclaimed, "Melchior was the name of one of the Three Wise Men, am I not correct?"

Again, the guests grinned and nodded their assent.

"Actually," Antek continued with a nod and in a rather pompous tone, "he also is believed to be the Wise Man who presented gold to the Christ Child. Of course, you know, I'm sure, that his associates contributed their own offerings of myrrh and frankincense." At the conclusion of the sentence, Philadelphia's Antek paused as if awaiting a brief round of applause.

"Correct again, dear bishop," Henry said, toasting his coffee cup toward the cleric. "And, I would be negligent not to mention," he added, with a smile, "Melchior Charitable Trust has a significant allotment of gold in its substantial portfolio. In fact," he paused and caught the eyes of the others, "it is appropriate for me to state that our entire existence and operation are built upon a rather unique and out-of-the-ordinary bedrock foundation involving significant *golden* assets."

The twinkling eyes of the two clerical cousins met as they exchanged avaricious smiles.

"Well, time is a bit short, and our Christmas week clock is ticking away," Antek said, interrupting. "Therefore, we would ask that you proceed directly to the purpose of your visit."

"Of course, Your Excellency," Henry replied, noting the abrupt manner in which their host had ended the welcoming pleasantries.

Unable to contain his greed-generated excitement, Maryland's Roman Branko growled a few comments that made the others react by clearing their throats. "Am I correct in recalling that you initially had mentioned a seven figure donation to each of our respective domains, I believe?" he asked. "And, I would like to add, I strongly hope that these funds are *unrestricted*—which, as I am sure you realize, allows us the utmost flexibility to distribute the assets to those poor, clueless unfortunates who have been placed in our charge. Since they cannot make wise decisions for themselves, it is for us to determine which are most in need and truly deserving." He completed his hopeful comment with a weak, fish-eyed grin.

Joey exchanged a knowing glance with Henry, who began their presentation. He mentioned the desire on the part of Mr. Novak to save the two provinces an amount exceeding $6 million.

Upon hearing the healthy nature of the figure, both hosts offered appreciative nods. Without a doubt, Santa Claus had made a surprise visit ahead of schedule.

Stan and Ollie could hardly contain their delight. While the skinny Philadelphia host rubbed his palms together briskly, the bigger Marylander nodded his multiple chins, bobbing them up and down several times. Visions of how to spend their holiday season windfall were happily dancing like sugarplums in their money-hungry heads.

Overwhelmed by the large figure Henry had tossed into the air, both capitalistic clerics missed the most important word in the visiting accountant's announcement—*save*.

At that point Joey knew he was in complete control and that the greedy hosts would agree to any demand, sign any document, perform any deed he stipulated. It was the same sense of confidence he had experienced that first night, when he was driving home after leaving Isadore Bloom's apartment and ran over the dog. Joey knew he could bring that puppy back to life for the little girl. At this moment, he knew that their lust for power would blind his two obnoxious targets. And Joey was going to savor the moment when his prey began to squirm and realize things were not going to go their way.

An obvious question presented by the Philadelphia cleric pulled Joey's attention back to the conversation.

"If I may convey a paramount inquiry," Antek/Stan interjected, "what, pray tell, is the impetus for your most unbridled munificence?"

Joey ignored the question, leaned over and whispered into Henry's ear, causing the two cousins to exchange quizzical glances.

Henry forced a smile. He knew the convivial atmosphere was about to change direction. Within the next few moments, the up-to-now pleasant mood was going to flee the room and, as they used to say, *head South*.

"Mr. Novak," Henry answered, "has instructed me to tell you he prefers that you speak in plain English, and not address him like you were attending a stuffy meeting of the Symphony Society or Polo Club board of directors. While a wealthy man, he is simple and direct in his tastes, conversations and business dealings."

A gray cloud of annoyance fell over the room like a wet shroud, but both clerics knew they could not afford to react in an aggravated fashion. Such action could derail the direction of the meeting and affect their possession of the millions of dollars that was still on the table, waiting to be grabbed.

"Thomas Manning," Henry said, bringing the conversation back to its focus and hoping to generate a reaction from the cousins.

Silence reigned for about ten long seconds as bold question marks appeared on Stan's and Ollie's faces. Without a doubt, a dead skunk had just been tossed onto the expensive antique table. But neither of the men gave any sign they were going to acknowledge its putrid smell.

"Gentlemen, please," Henry said, urging them to search the ancient storage areas of their brains. "Certainly Your Excellencies recall the name and circumstances surrounding your involvement in the sordid affair of Reverend Thomas Manning."

While Roman shifted ever so slightly, but uncomfortably, in his overstuffed chair, Antek rose and moved away from the group. He stopped at the window, ignoring the others. His angry face was gazing down on the well-manicured courtyard.

"Let me refresh some faded memories, then," Henry said. "St. Romonius' Church. Slightly more than seven years ago."

A flash of scarlet seared across Roman Branko's face. Using all his energy, he forced himself to lift his large frame out of the chair and stomped onto the floor, heading toward his cousin. Visibly shaking, he turned and sputtered, "What is the meaning of this outrage?"

Smiling, Joey nodded to Henry, urging him to continue.

"Ah. I see you haven't suffered a complete memory loss," the accountant said. "Now, I will move the story along, as it seems your dear cousin, Antek, hasn't had any chimes go off in his bell tower as of yet. Remember the two altar boys, Mark Schaeffer and William Aube? A rather unpleasant incident occurred within the St. Romonius' Church sacristy, following an early morning Mass. I believe the disturbance involved doctored wine, a bloody shirt and a subsequent cover-up. Bishop Antek, do you have any thoughts on the subject, and the rash actions of both you and your cousin?"

The host turned back from the window and glared at the guests, who had suddenly become unwelcome intruders. "Old business," he said through a clenched jaw. "Taken care of satisfactorily many years ago. Not relevant and, frankly, none of your damn business. So if that is why you two are here, I think it's best for all involved that you both leave, *immediately*!"

Roman, who had feared the incident would someday resurface, tried to remained composed. He hovered beside his cousin near the window, placing as much distance as possible between himself and the still seated accusing guests.

"I'm afraid we can't do that, quite yet, Your Excellencies," Henry said, opening a number of documents from his folders and, finally, pulling a bloody shirt, sealed in clear plastic, from his satchel.

Before the accountant could continue, Antek shouted, "I've had enough of this nonsense!" The host suddenly began to move toward his desk, intending to press the emergency security buzzer, which was located in an indentation to the right of his center drawer.

But Joey read his thoughts and froze the auxiliary bishop in place. The man's legs would not move. His body was unable to process the directions being sent by his clearly malfunctioning brain. Shocked, the cleric grunted, trying to will his body to respond, but it wouldn't budge. Roman, the plump one, raised both hands near his mouth, exhibiting definite fear. Acting as if he would catch a communicable disease, he quickly moved a half-dozen steps away from his now statuesque cousin.

Henry and Joey took the opportunity to place six stacks of paper alongside each other on the top of Antek's massive mahogany desk.

When they ran out of space, Joey made more room by pushing the auxiliary bishop's in-box onto the floor, scattering his personal papers in several directions.

The two guests ignored their temporarily frozen host. Joey turned toward the terrified still-mobile cousin—who was mumbling cryptic phrases and words, among them "demons," "demonic possession" and "servants of Satan."

Snapping his fingers at Roman, Joey directed the big man to pay close attention, explaining they had come to address the criminal assault on the boy and the calculated destruction of Thomas Manning's clerical career. Their actions seven years earlier could result in a costly civil lawsuit and a significant amount of negative publicity.

Henry held up affidavits signed by both boys involved in the incident, their parents and Rev. Randy Heckbert. He was the province representative who, at the time, had dismissed the police officers and initiated the cover-up at Auxiliary Bishop Antek Branko's direction.

"We found your former associate, Reverend Heckbert, at a mission church near Princess Anne, Maryland," Henry said. "He wasn't hesitant to tell us how upset he has been, after being deposited in that no man's land. At the mention of your names, he indicated he would do anything to get even with you both. Apparently, you've ignored his correspondence and passed him over for promotion a number of times." Shaking his head, Henry added, "You know what they say, Your Excellencies: *Revenge is a dish best served cold*. It's apparent your long-forgotten friend, Heckbert, has been waiting patiently to even the score."

"What do you want?" snapped Antek, still stiff and quite annoyed at the situation.

"Only a few little signatures," Joey said, speaking in a calm but confident voice that seemed to ignore Antek's irritated tone. "We have come to *save* you millions, not *give* you millions. However, this meeting will not be without serious costs to you both."

Neither nervous cleric replied.

"And, since you would be much more comfortable seated, I can release you from that awkward position," Joey said. "But if you get upset and begin thinking about touching that security buzzer, I'll place both of you in an immobile state. Follow me?"

No immediate reply.

"Last chance, Antek, my friend," Joey said, flashing a false smile.

Antek nodded and, when Joey looked at Roman, the larger man nodded rapidly, indicating he agreed even more profusely.

With a bow of his head, Joey released Antek's muscles from bondage and, using his mind, ordered the pair to retake their seats. When they had complied, Henry continued giving instructions, detailing the master plan for Father Manning's retribution and the clerical cousins' human salvation.

To avoid a $4 million judgment against the Northeastern Province, and a more than $2 million similar action against St. Brendan the Navigator's Seminary, the two clergy would agree to:

° Reinstate Rev. Thomas Manning, promote him to prelate and allow him to select a rector position at any church in the province,

° Compensate him monetarily with $150,000, which includes back pay and pain and suffering—which was described as "a bargain" based on the humiliation the currently inactive priest had endured, and

° Invite Prelate Manning to concelebrate Christmas Eve Mass at the Cathedral of St. Bogdan, this evening, and also present the sermon.

At that point, Philly's Antek snarled, "Why can't your friend Manning give the damn sermon in Annapolis, in Roman's area of the province? He's the blithering idiot that got us into this mess."

Slowly shaking his head from side to side, Joey gave a disappointed look and said, "Oh, I don't think so, Antek. Prelate Manning wouldn't like to travel that far. But, you know what? Maybe *you* could ride down I-95 and do that, instead. I'm sure Roman here would be glad to welcome you at his place tonight. Afterwards, you two could sit around the seminary fireplace and share fond memories, talk about old times, your schemes and dreams of better Christmases, now long gone and never to return."

Roman was totally confused and trying to catch a sympathetic glance from anyone who might happen to look his way.

Taking the silence and lack of continued protest as a signs of agreement, Henry carried on with his list of demands. "You also will:

"Apologize to Prelate Manning this evening, before Mass. You, of course, will stay to do this as well, Roman. And by the first of March, you both will retire from your positions in the church and take no other authoritative roles where you will be involved with religious personnel. Essentially, you will be exiled to your private homes or a monastery or retreat house of your choosing."

Joey knew the two men, who were considered for archbishop positions, wouldn't be able to handle the final demand. He sat back, waiting to see which cousin would be the first to explode.

Antek didn't let him down.

"Who the hell do you think you are? Coming in here, and strong arming us, as if we are nothing more than common criminals. You begin by baiting us with the promise of money, and then you think you are going to steal us blind. Let me tell you this," Antek's anger was heading off the chart, "there are laws against . . . ."

"THANK YOU! THANK YOU! THANK YOU!" Joey shouted as he leapt from his chair. "I was hoping you wouldn't agree. See Henry," Joey looked toward his associate, "I told you they would put up a fight. Great! Now, get on the phone and tell the press they can open the juicy information we had sent to them but had embargoed until our call."

Turning to face Antek and Roman, Joey said, "Do you know what a slow news night this is? Christmas Eve? Same old stuff every year. People helping the poor. Cops and nurses working through the overnight shift. People opening presents. Dull, dull, dull. But, if we're speaking of presents, you two big boys are going to give the parasites in the newsrooms their year-end bonuses. Your story will make the noon, 6 and 11 o'clock TV reports, and you'll be on the front page on Christmas Day morning!"

"You can't do this," Roman muttered.

Laughing, Joey raced over and looked directly into the heavy cleric's face. "You overweight moron, we already have. Those press releases are in the hands of couriers at this moment. And one of our messengers is at City Hall, where your archbishop will be concluding a meeting with the mayor in about 15 minutes. Of course, I'm sure he has no idea of the Manning fiasco and your roles in it. Correct, Antek?" Joey turned, shifting his gaze in the direction of the other deflated and defeated cleric. "Imagine what he'll do when he gets his early surprise Christmas revelation about you two?"

No one spoke, so Joey continued, "This information," he stressed, "will be delivered as soon as Henry gives the word. The press release has every juicy detail of the cover-up and beating of the altar boys."

When the Brankos did not reply, Joey turned to his accountant and asked, "Tell me the truth, Henry. How many times have you ever seen a 'PRIEST POUNDS ALTAR BOY IN THE FACE' story across page one on Christmas morning?"

Henry shook his head, indicating he had no idea.

"How about you guys?" Joey asked, looking at the dejected cousins. "Ever heard of a story like that on the holiest day of the year?"

The duo was silent, their bodies limp, their minds racing through their options, which boiled down to one—unconditional surrender.

"And don't forget the $6 million in lawsuits and the interviews with your angry flunky priest, who you idiots exiled to the Middle of Nowhere, Maryland. Then we bring out poor Tom Manning, who you two asses royally screwed out of SEVEN YEARS OF HIS LIFE!"

Suddenly, Joey wasn't mocking them anymore. His tone shrill. He was losing control. His face a mask of unrestrained anger and disgust. He faced them and snarled, "You two rotten pieces of crap have destroyed a man's life, sucked the spirit out of his soul. If you don't agree to everything we have on these papers, and sign them right now, I'm going to spend every penny of my fortune to see that you both are humiliated and shunned until you are dumped in a hole in the ground on your dying day.

"Think of me as your vengeful angel of retribution—sort of a living St. Michael with a sharp spear I intend to shove up your fat bottoms. I was sent here to take you both down, to deliver your penance in person. Now, get up off your fat behinds and let's get this over with. We have more respectable people to deal with today."

After Roman and Antek completed signing the agreements, Henry gave them each a copy and placed the rest of the papers, and the bloody shirt, into his leather bag.

As Joey reached the door, he turned and said, "Reverend, I mean *Prelate*, Manning will be here at 10 o'clock tonight. You'll have a nice catered meal, with the good stuff set out for him. And get him a fancy new cassock—one of those tailored ones you bigshots wear—plus a list of all your churches, so he can pick the one he wants. Oh, I'll be here, along with my wife, son and a half-dozen friends. We'll all go to Mass, at St. Bogdan's Cathedral, in the front rows, of course, planning on listening to his sermon. So you will reserve those seats for us, right?"

Neither man bothered to reply. Joey knew they would do anything he said.

"Finally," sounding a bit bored with the ordeal, Joey added, "don't even think of delaying your resignations. If they aren't announced by March 1, this information gets released and the lawsuits will fly. Understand, *Your Excellencies*?"

The men nodded weakly, indicating resigned agreement.

"Great," Joey said, suddenly opening his arms, plastering a broad smile across his face, and adding, "Oh, I almost forgot. Merry Christmas! God bless us every one!"

CHAPTER 30

Midnight Mass

Following Father Tom's reception at the province's office, Joey, Janice, JJ, Long John, Donna and a few of the girls from the diner—along with Uncle Lou, Jersey Jack, and even Buddah and Buddy Bassdard—sat in the reserved front pews of the cathedral.

The ex-priest's reinstatement party was a success, and any casual observer would have thought the two religious bigshots and Tom Manning were long lost roommates.

With her arm entwined in her husband's, Janice leaned over and whispered, "So when did Tom find out he was giving the sermon tonight?"

Joey turned and smiled. "About 11:30 this morning," he whispered. "He's been a nervous wreck all day. Been practicing it at the Inn on everybody. He even wanted to head over to the diner and try it out with Donna and the girls."

"Good thing you held him back," Janice said, laughing softly.

Directing Janice toward the other guests in their pew with a thrust of his chin, Joey said, "Look, they all have copies with corrections marked on them. They'll be able to read along with him when he starts talking."

After a few moments, Janice pulled JJ, who was seated to her right and placed him in between her and Joey.

Rubbing his son's head, Joey thought how he had originally wished that his son would be able to hear, that he would be able to cure him. But in the last several weeks Joey also realized how lucky his family was, how happy they could be when they appreciated all that they had been given, not what they didn't have.

There was still about 15 minutes before the entry procession, when the church would be cloaked in darkness, except for the glow of scores of candlelights, flickering through the aisles.

Janice leaned over and told her husband, "I love you very much."

Joey looked in her dark, captivating eyes. "Me, too."

As the Mass progressed they sat in silence, reciting prayers, singing carols and recalling Christmases past. While listening to the newly reinstated priest's sermon, Joey was struck by the message of unconditional love and forgiveness that Tom, who had endured so much, had extended to all present. Joey was sure the good priest's unselfish comments even included honest goodwill toward those who had abused their power and made his life a misery for so many years. It was more than Joey would have been able to do. *But*, Joey thought, *rebirth, love and forgiveness are the true messages of Christ's birthday*.

"I guess you could say Tom is your first Christmas miracle," Janice whispered. "He looks so happy tonight. You should be very proud."

"Thankful," Joey said. "Yeah, thankful, I think that's a better word to describe how I feel right now."

Looking in his eyes, Janice paused and said, "How about two Christmas miracles? Can you handle that, my love?"

Joey paused, trying to read her mind. But the Keeper's power couldn't break down the wall guarding Janice's special secret. "What do you mean?"

Laughing, she said, "I can't believe you can't guess, that you don't know."

Suddenly, Joey's eyes glistened like sparkling gems, and his face was consumed by a growing smile. "You're not? Are you?"

Nodding, Janice said, "Yes, Joey. Yes! We're going to have a baby. I just found out yesterday. I thought this was the best place to tell you. The timing just seemed perfect."

And it was, for as Joey pulled his wife closer to share an embrace, all of the lights in the church went off. But in Joey and Janice's eyes, bright starlight shone, a sign that they had received a Christmas miracle that even the Keeper of the Coins alone could not have arranged.

Chapter 31

Jan. 6, Feast of the Three Kings

In *Webster's New World Dictionary*, the word Epiphany has several meanings, among them: An appearance or manifestation of a god or some other supernatural being; in many Christian churches, a yearly festival, held January 6, commemorating both the revealing of Jesus as the Christ to the Gentiles in the persons of the Magi or Three Kings; and a moment of sudden intuitive understanding or a flash of insight.

Other than the recent attendance at Father Tom's Christmas service, for the first time in years, Joey went to Mass at St. Hedwig's on the Feast of the Epiphany, with Janice and JJ.

Knowing that he had a very close connection to Gaspar, Melchior and Balthazar made the Mass and incense ceremony that followed quite special. It was Joey's first January 6 since his meeting with Isadore Bloom. That encounter had changed his life, as well as that of his family, friends and countless strangers in need.

In his mind, it was fitting on this feast day, in particular, that he reflect on his life—where he had been and the long road he would be traveling. It was good for Joey to dwell on these matters in such a quiet and holy place.

Of course, the rest of the day was spent taking down ornaments and decorations. Christmas season was officially over. The Three Wise Men, the Three Kings, had arrived, bearing their distinctive gifts.

It was snowing steadily as Janice packed the family's small and large Christmas treasures into familiar dented cardboard boxes. Soon they would be hauled into the cellar and stored away until next year.

Joey stood on a stepstool at the front door. He was performing an annual ritual that had been a custom in his family and that of millions of other Eastern Europeans for centuries. Taking chalk that had been blessed that morning at the conclusion of Mass, he printed the letters K + M + B—the initials of the Three Kings—followed by the year, above each first-floor entrance doorway of his house.

"It's a tradition, so that we'll be protected from harm, and that only those with good will and kind intentions will come into our home this year," he told Janice the first time he had performed the custom. As years passed, the action had become more cultural than religious, but still Joey carefully drew the chalk markings, boasting he had never missed a year.

Placing the ladder in front of the last door, the one in the kitchen at the rear of the house, he thought of the good things he had been blessed to be a part of. Father Tom had been promoted to prelate and was rector of a wonderful little church in Lancaster County, less than a two-hour drive from the city. Tony C quit the police force and was working as a security consultant for the Melchior Charitable Trust. Donna and the girls were working well in their diner. That decision by Janice turned out to be a success. Plans were continuing on the new wing at the children's hospital. Alex, the fellow who found employment through Melinda's music talk show, had worked out so well that Henry was planning a promotion party. Shelley's kidney was functioning well, and there were scores of other folks who had benefited from the Keeper's attention.

Most importantly, JJ lived at home with his parents, not needing to be sent far away from home for schooling.

Joey stood on the third step of the metal ladder, paused a moment and said a quick silent prayer of thanks, offering a kindly thought for Isadore Bloom. His mentor had saved Janice's life and provided Joey guidance and support. How he missed the old guy, but Joey knew Izzy would appear again, when least expected.

Wiping a tear from his eye, Joey lost his grip on the blessed piece of chalk, which fell to the tile floor with a distinctive piercing ding.

Suddenly, as he turned to look for its location, Joey noticed that JJ, who had been writing at the kitchen table, lifted his head sharply, his eyes frantically searching the room.

Thinking he was imagining the unimaginable, Joey took a pen out of his pocket and dropped it on the tile floor. The sound this time was not as high pitched, but still noticeable.

Joey watched his son carefully. He began to sense a growing nervousness when JJ shifted his head, and then slowly moved his left hand to his ear. With confusion displayed across his face, the young boy looked up toward his father and softly said, "Dad?"

Amazed that his lips had caused a sound that he, himself, could hear, JJ said it again, looking directly at his father's eyes. "Dad?"

Shocked, his heart beating rapidly, Joey moved his body deliberately down the steps of the ladder. He didn't want to wish for too much. He was afraid to let his mind run away with crazy ideas, dreams that he knew could not come true. He also didn't want to scare his son, who might possibly be hearing sounds for the very first time in his life.

Stopping in front of the table, Joey looked at JJ, took his son's hands, knelt down and asked slowly and softly, in a quiet whisper, "JJ, can you hear me? If so, just nod your head."

Praying that this was real, not a dream, Joey nodded his own head slowly while watching his son's every move. He later realized he was almost crushing the boy's hands as the nervous youngster nodded rapidly and smiled at his father.

Telling JJ to stay where he was and promise not to move an inch, Joey ran into the basement, his eyes filling with tears. He struggled to maintain his composure as he shouted for Janice, calling his wife's name three times. Gently, but swiftly, he took her by the arm and directed her up the cellar stairs toward their waiting son.

Ignoring her questions and keeping his face out of view, Joey stopped her at the top step, at the opening of the basement door. Walking into the kitchen, Joey told Janice to wait as he took JJ across the room and situated him so his back faced his parents.

Running back to his wife, Joey said, "Now call out his name," urging Janice to speak.

"Is this a joke, Joey? Did you two arrange some kind of game or secret signal?" Her annoyance was apparent.

"Please, Jan," Joey pleaded, trying to remain calm, "just do it. Call to him."

But before she could utter a word, JJ spoke, while looking at the opposite wall. "It's true, Mom. I . . . can hear. I can hear you both!"

And the laughing boy turned around and rushed toward his mother, who embraced him in her arms. Joey followed and joined the group, sweeping them both off their feet. Then they all sat on the floor, hugging and crying and laughing. And Joey, Janice and JJ savored an unexpected gift that was much more valuable than Gold, Frankincense or Myrrh.

Epilogue

Joey still works at the Welcome Inn, although that isn't the real name of the establishment. If we shared its actual identity, the place would be mobbed by saints and schemers, religious fanatics and historians, and curiosity seekers and television producers. Also, Joey Novak isn't the moniker of the present Keeper of the Coins. We couldn't tell you that either.

But it's true a special wing in a children's hospital has been dedicated in the name of the Keeper's wife, not only in the town where they live but also in many cities throughout the world.

The precious and powerful Three Kings' coins are safely hidden, many believe in a safety deposit box, but certainly not in a buried coffee can. They're waiting to be transferred to the next person who will serve as their guardian and use their powers for good.

One day, sometime in the future, an average, apparently insignificant person—with a good soul and a kind heart—will find the hidden key, open the box and read Joey's letter.

In the meantime, there are many—including, perhaps you—who will continue to watch for clues of the present Keeper's activity.

These hints or signs might appear as a small, filler-type story in a large daily newspaper—about a minor miracle that science can't explain. Or on the evening news, when a reporter spotlights the tale of a passing stranger who rescues a troubled family from harm. There might be a report about a mysterious benefactor, who purchases a forsaken company in a small town and saves the dying community by preserving hundreds of jobs—or there may be a story about expensive jewels, or hundred-dollar bills, mysteriously appearing in dented red kettles at Christmastime.

The next Keeper is out there, but we'll never know who it is. Only one person—his or her successor—will learn the identity.

You see, that's the way it's always been, and that's the way it has to be.

When they saw the star,
they rejoiced with exceeding great joy.
And when they came into the house,
they saw the young child
with Mary his mother,
and fell down, and worshiped him:
and when they had opened their treasures,
they presented unto him gifts:
gold, frankincense and myrrh.

THE END

About the Author

Ed Okonowicz is a storyteller and regional author. He presents programs in schools, theaters, libraries and public and private sites throughout the Mid-Atlantic Region. In 2005 he was named Best Local Author in the *Delaware Today* magazine annual Readers' Poll, and he has appeared on The Learning Channel programs. As an adjunct instructor, he teaches folklore, storytelling and writing at the University of Delaware, where he worked as a writer and editor. He and his wife, Kathleen—an accomplished watercolor artist and graphic designer—own Myst and Lace Publishers, Inc.

Visit the web site at **www.mystandlace.com**

To order a copy of *Gold, Frankincense and Myrrh* to share with a friend—or for information on other books offered by Myst and Lace Publishers, Inc.—use the order form on page 156 or visit the web site: **www.mystandlace.com**

Myst and Lace Publishers, Inc.

A sampling of our titles

Ghost Stories

Regional Ghosts and History

Novels and Love Stories

Oral History

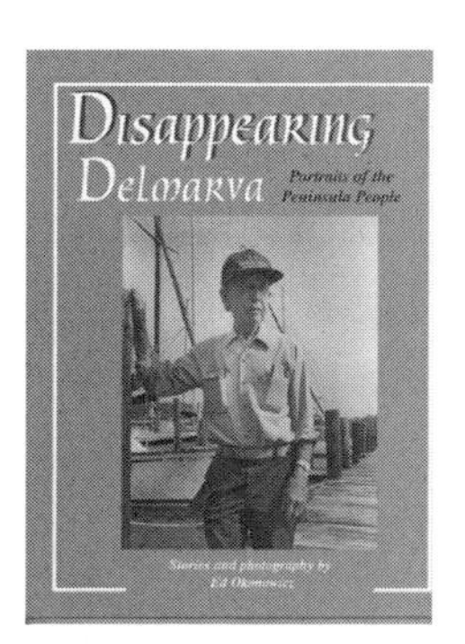

To Order our Books

Name____

Address______________________________________

City____________________State______Zip___________

Phone__(_____)___________e-mail____________________

To receive our free newsletter nd information on future books, public tours and events, send us your e-mail address, visit our web site [www.mystandlace.com] or fill out the above form and mail it to us.

I would like to order the following books:

Quantity	Title	Price	Total
______	**Gold, Frankincense & Myrrh**	**$ 11.95**	______
______	Annapolis Ghosts	$ 11.95	______
______	Haunted Maryland	$ 9.95	______
______	Civil War Ghosts at Fort Delaware	$ 11.95	______
______	Baltimore Ghosts	$ 11.95	______
______	Baltimore Ghosts Teacher's Guide	$ 8.95	______
______	Lighthouses of Maryland and Virginia	$ 11.95	______
______	Lighthouses of New Jersey and Delaware	$ 11.95	______
______	Terrifying Tales of the Beaches and Bays	$ 9.95	______
______	Terrifying Tales 2 of the Beaches and Bays	$ 9.95	______
______	Treasure Hunting	$ 6.95	______
______	Opening the Door Vol II (second edition)	$ 9.95	______
______	In the Vestibule, Vol IV	$ 9.95	______
______	Presence in the Parlor, Vol V	$ 9.95	______
______	Crying in the Kitchen, Vol VI	$ 9.95	______
______	Up the Back Stairway, Vol VII	$ 9.95	______
______	Horror in the Hallway, Vol VIII	$ 9.95	______
______	Phantom in the Bedchamber, Vol IX	$ 9.95	______
______	Possessed Possessions	$ 9.95	______
______	Possess Possessions 2	$ 9.95	______
______	Ghosts	$ 9.95	______
______	Fired! A DelMarVa Murder Mystery (DMM)	$ 9.95	______
______	Halloween House	$ 9.95	______
______	Disappearing Delmarva	$ 38.00	______
______	Friends, Neighbors & Folks Down the Road	$ 30.00	______
______	Stairway over the Brandywine, A Love Story	$ 5.00	______

Subtotal________

Tax* ________

Shipping ________

Total________

*Md residents add 5% sales tax.
Please include $ 2.50 postage for the first book, and 50 cents for each additional book.
Make checks payable to: Myst and Lace Publishers

All books are signed by the author. If you would like the book(s) personalized, please specify to whom. Mail to: Ed Okonowicz
1386 Fair Hill Lane
Elkton, Maryland 21921

 Visit our web site at: www.mystandlace.com